# The Marriage Hearse

### A Novel By
## Larry Duberstein

But most thro' midnight streets I hear
How the youthful Harlots curse
Blasts the new-born Infants tear
And blights with plagues the Marriage Hearse
— William Blake

THE PERMANENT PRESS

To Lee

| | |
|---|---|
| ILLUSTRATIONS | Dorothy Ahle |
| CALLIGRAPHY | Jamie Duberstein |
| TYPOGRAPHY | Cass von Braun |

Library of Congress Number: 86-062450
International Standard Book Number: 0-932966-76-4

Manufactured in the United States of America

THE PERMANENT PRESS
RD2 Noyac Road
Sag Harbor, NY 11963

# LIST OF ILLUSTRATIONS

It is not true that love makes
all things easy: it makes us
choose what is difficult.

— George Eliot

Love hinders death.

— Leo Tolstoy

# THE OUTSET

This story will begin with a simple scene in which a middle-aged man is strolling home after his day at the office and chooses to stop an hour or so at a neighborhood tavern for a glass of ale. But it will not begin quite yet, for that man is myself, Maurice Locksley, and because you no doubt know me through my other books there is something I would take the liberty of saying right at the outset. In fact, it occurs to me now that there are dozens of things I could say right at the outset. How long is an outset, anyway? We might stretch a point and get all our business transacted "right at the outset".

But the story, if and when it begins, will cover the time span between 5:00 p.m. on December 19 and 3:39 a.m. on the morning, technically, of December 20. The weather will be "variable" and the locale will shift from the city of Boston to some of its outlying villages and then back again, as we follow that hero of so much modern literature "I" in a ten hour and thirty-nine minute pursuit of himself. Who is "I"? (Who am I?) And who is this "himself" that he is forever pursuing, what makes the fellow flee and hide?

What I did wish to say right at the outset, however, is that I personally have never liked writing in what is called the first person, by which is meant not Adam but "I", this same "I" who invariably talks too much and mostly, almost obsessively, about "himself". You will ransack the ouevre in vain if you are looking to find a story of any substance by Maurice

Locksley in the first person, for this is my first, and therefore his. That breadth of address, all those digressions and wry flourishes of the "gentle reader" ilk, such liberties of affectation are just so many soft shoulders along the high road of narrative. And yet I have concluded after much consideration that in this case, that person, the first, is the lesser of evils as there might be even greater affectation in the instance of a writer writing about a writer that is himself, in the third person. Do you not agree? □

So yes, "I" will reluctantly be telling my story and as a direct result you and I must both expect to make certain sacrifices. There will likewise be benefits derived, for already I feel closer to you than I might have and I'll wager you come to feel the same way if you remain with me to the end. And if you have remained with me at least to the beginning, that moment is now at hand.

# Loose Time

**W**illiam Faulkner, himself a writer, once offered some advice on the subject of wives. He said the trick was to keep the first one and simply try to outlast her.

Good wry words from a pithy small-town man who valued his leisure, his ramblings and his ruminations, his pipe and his bourbon, and above all his work. A man must have his range and be at home on it, and to continually muddy the waters of priority with questions of the *heart* would surely take much away from the peace and quiet of life. If a man will go strewing sons and lovers, wives and daughters about the map, slicing his time and scattering his money, he may very well find there is little of either left for "himself".

I am pondering Faulkner's advice, and how it bears upon my own situation, as I pace off the seven blocks between my office and my home, at 5:00 p.m. on the already dark afternoon of December 19, 19––. And thus preoccupied I have paid scarcely any notice to the stream of Bostonians flowing past me, or to the dozens of shop windows layed out to entice me, until I happen to glance up just in front of a bar called Bourbon-on-the-Charles and, alternatively, The Sportsman's Paradise. You see, the place has two names, two signs hung one above the other, over the door. The Bourbon-on-the-Charles sign is higher and larger, while The Sportsman's Paradise glows out from below in midnight-blue neon, so it really is impossible to choose between them.

I have gone past this tavern some two thousand times and it would surprise you I am sure the amount of time I have spent on the question of nomenclature. According to my current theory, The Sportsman's Paradise was here first, a neighborhood fixture, and simply merged some years back with another bar called Bourbon-on-the-Charles that must originally have stood in somewhat greater proximity to the banks of the Charles River, which runs between Boston and Cambridge out to sea. Until two years ago I had held staunchly to a completely different theory, in which the owner could not decide finally between his two favorite names, and so had decided to keep them both. And being an original fellow, he was bothered not at all by the geographical imprecision of one of those names. The place is listed in the phone book, if you were wondering, under neither name.

Of course I could at any time have ascertained the truth very easily—half of me yearns for that simple explanation even as the other half shrinks from such deflation and would forever revel in theories instead—but in fact I have never set foot inside the bar. Never once, either to research my theories or to slake my palatine desires, though I stroll past it no less than twice a day and have always been drawn to the place. And yet the split-second I glance up at the two signs, and at the large front window which I know for a fact is divided into exactly forty-eight panes of glass, I know also that I will be going inside today.

Never tempted at 9:00 a.m. when the door is propped ajar and the stools peacefully inhabited by the l'âge d'or set, or after lunch when it shelters the able-bodied unemployed, I had often envied the crowd I saw in there around quitting time, now, the ones who had finished a day's labor and had some loose time, pub time, in which to unwind before the wending homeward. It is a tradesman's bar at this hour and clearly houses that stout fellow whose work and whose comrades rate

slightly higher than his home and family, mates over mate, for
reasons never understood or even explored. But I, Maurice
Locksley, am also moving through the portal to lift a glass or
two inside and ever the relentless analyst, never content to
leave such matters under-examined, I am asking myself *why* I
am here before I fully clear the threshold.

1) Because it was there. Well this is certainly true, on-
tology notwithstanding, and yet it cannot be the correct
answer because it was also "there" on the two thousand prior
occasions.

2) Because if I did not go in, and went directly home instead, to Kim and gentle Ben, I might then have to resent
Kim or Ben, potentially warping the latter (age four) or irking
the former (age thirty-seven). Not good to warp the young,
not wise to irk the middle-aged; not even sound to resent, for
the self itself can warp or crack.

Here I interrupt my analysis, though by no means ruling
out 2) entirely, and make safari through the thick grove of
smoke and hearty splashing cheer to the bar. I select a stool
(the last one free) and also a tone in which to voice my
preference for Bass Ale (strong silent flat western), then settle
back into normal voice by way of accepting a domestic
mediocrity instead. Rinsing my mouth with said mediocrity I
am able to rule out

3) Because I had conceived a thirst of such magnitude as to
permit no further perambulation prior to quenchment: the
oasis syndrome. This is not the case. I wanted the element
more than the aliment, the glass more than its contents. For
one does require the glass in a bar-room. It is the chief prop in-
animate but also in subtle ways one socializes with it. Were it
not for the glass, one might easily appear lost, or lonely, out
of place; with it, always busy and belonging. So I am "in
place", not as it were déglassé, and free to plunge ahead to a
consideration of

4) Because today is a unique and special day. Now that is good. In fact that might be it, for isn't this the day I have chosen to tell you about—not three years ago Saturday or Tuesday week, but *today*—and so it must indeed be special, mustn't it?

Though I have never been inside Bourbon-on-the-Charles before, I see much that looks familiar. Many of the neighborhood faces are here, faces I have smiled into and even greeted, yet never known at all, and the mise-en-scène is common enough. Wall decorations incline to the sportsman's paradise theme: Ted Williams landing a fish, Luis Tiant checking his baserunners, Bobby Orr scoring a goal to win the Stanley Cup. The lighting is pleasant, a shaded amber lantern on the wall by each dark wooden booth, and the bartender has been narrating a suitably worldly anecdote to a crew of carpenters about a remodeling job he once did himself, for the longshoreman's union in Charleston, South Carolina. (The union had elected to finance the conversion of a café next door to the union hall into a bawdyhouse, and the job had mainly consisted of buying some red light-bulbs and exterminating the rats in the cellar.)

The carpenters laugh at the story, as does everyone else within earshot. Most of the patrons here are tradespeople, in trios and pairs, sipping at glasses of draught beer. One fellow who came in red-faced and raging, haranguing a lad who is likely both his son and his helper, has grown mellower by the glass till he now seems as sweet and cheerful as a brandywine friar. Another pair sits in absolute stony silence; the tall red-haired one with "Cliff" lettered on his shirt-pocket flap, grins a bit from time to time and every once in a while, for no discernible reason, his whole face flushes brightly and the grin faintly broadens. Then he nods to his buddy, still without speaking, and sips more beer.

BOURBON-ON-THE-CHARLES

There are more. Every table contains a vignette, relationships and eccentricities, and I am fascinated by this as always. In the corner by the billiard table, three plumbers share a pitcher of dark beer. One of them relates a tale of vengeance against a late-paying customer, his phrasing in cadence with the click and roll of the billiard balls. "Don't get mad," he works his refrain with flawless stand-up style and timing, "Just get even." His table-mates, much younger men, alternately follow his story and carry forth a separate story of their own, regarding a mutual acquaintance with "huge tits".

New clients wedge themselves into the room and though I take passing notice of each, I note one threesome in particular, as was no doubt fated. My curse. The three are painters, got up as painters at any rate, two tall young men and a woman roughly twenty-five, with long black hair and a startling long white body. This is no child, this is an Eligible, someone who will clearly require "elimination" and by this I certainly do not mean what the Mob or Central Intelligence might mean by it, but rather that if this extraordinary person is to be excluded from my life, I must demand to know *why*, on what basis.

She has the grace to be wearing her painter's whites a size large, withal the posterior to make them snug and unwrinkled at the seat. Long muscular legs, presumably on the scheme of her long muscular arms, and a gently bobbing breast-line inside the soft faded cotton work-shirt. It is hard to stop looking at her face: deep green eyes, the curving smile, and rich smooth skin, all played out in a succession of charming expressions for the most acute and discerning audience. This is somebody's dream girl, most likely one of the two spattered gentlemen currently flanking her. She is sharing a glass with the bearded one and yet he lacks the proprietary air... In fact, ye Gods and little fishes, he is cruising over to the pinball machine, abandoning her there at table!

No doubt I've been staring like a stunned ox, but my mother wit has been busy all the while and now at last I believe I have it. Zap! She is eliminated. You see, I forgot in the sheer excitement of observing her (the writer's boon and bane) and yet it was right there all along: surfeit. The girl is excellent, intuition tells me her excellence is general. Excellent her hips, excellent her heart, everything about her uniformly excellent—share a plank with her anytime, like to work with m' hands too y' know—but then can she be any more excellent than Kim? Than Maggie Cornelius? Than Adele Blaney?

Though you will not meet these three estimable ladies until a bit later in the evening, you can take it from Locksley they are well-nigh matchless within their species and even allowing Green Eyes a similar status, she is eliminated by simple historical linearity and by the state of surfeit. Satis est. Scratch Green Eyes, then, ease her down from the swaying plank of imagination to restore some balance. And is it not worth a second mug of ale to have done so? But God *damn* it, Locksley, stop peeking at the clock, for there remains to be considered

5) Why *not* go inside? Maybe all we have here is just a leetle break-through in thinking, to look at the problem from the other side evidentially, burden-of-proofishly if you will. And what is the why-not? Well, generally the why-not takes the form of hurry. Hurry hurry. There is this rush, never fully defined but presumed to be part of the condition of Love, a heartfelt or headfelt obligation; rushing to women, rushing to children, they need to have us there.

So what about these folks here, looking squarely at six bells in Bourbon-on-the-Charles? (Yes, for purposes of narrative simplicity I have chosen between the two names, a feat which the proprietor himself proved unequal to, in my earlier theory.) But do they not suffer from the obligation to rush? Have they simply never incurred it, or do they choose most willfully to ignore it? And in any case, what makes for such a situation, whereby they lay easy claim to this loose time I seem to crave?

Maybe this is no more than a fly-by-night identity crisis for me, a career crisis really, for writing is after all a lonely trade, others seem so sociable by contrast, and I have been at it a long time. Perhaps I require a change, you check the level and I'll nail her off sort of change. Even as a child I played alone much of the time and now I have worked alone, all my life. Other lives, other jobs must be more fun. Even office work—all that yakking and flirting and coffee-breaking, betting pools and car pools and sly joking about spousies—well, maybe not office work but surely these others, the macho trades with their skill and pride and strength, pipes and wires and boards, beer and skittles... Why even a crummy piece of sheet-rock might be enough to make a man o' me!

Cause I'm forty now, see, and life seems largely gone by— but all of a *sudden* somehow—it seems chosen and used up, and I must wonder have I chosen well? Have I done the right things, in the right places, with the right people? Was there, for me, choice at all? (Don't recall making such. M.L.)

Almost immediately there is light. At once a mild epiphany, and I must remind you that this may be a night brimming with epiphanies large and small, that you must brace your credulity on this particular and special night. But now into our teeming sportsman's paradise from the dingy street outside come two brand new characters and the two combine to form something else new in our population, a couple. We have just acquired the classical heterosexual couple composed of one man and the abutting woman, he the higher by five inches, the heftier by fifty pounds, her hair the longer by a foot, arm in arm. Standardized model old-line heterosexual pairing, of bland description. What can *they* want?

Have they wandered in from the cold solely to remind me that indeed there was once choice, to recall to me that bygone era when birth was still controlled? For yes my darling children, there was such a time, and mom and dad roamed the globe alone, bereft of your sort (to what purpose, you may ask) and therefore unaccountable except possibly to each other. And was that easy? You bet it was. Precisely what it was, in fact, easy as pie. Drifting and dreaming, late après-midi fucking followed by re-run movies followed by cheapo restaurants and bars... The old arm-in-arm era! Was that fun? You bet it was.

It was 1965, Maurice Locksley, and you were in the prime of life when they tossed that little war in Southeast Asia. Forgotten that one? Best not forget, for that was it, that was your choice—housed within the choices already made for you by others, to be sure, but you did choose. There were other chancier roads open—exile, prison, the underground—but you pre-meditated a birth instead. In 1966 Will was born and you were "deferred", your death was put back while the deaths of certain others unknown to you personally were hastened forward in time.

Guilt for this? Not a bit of it, not then, not now. You would have gone to jail, to the bug-house, to Canada or Sweden; you played the game by the rules, too, just like the dead ones and the scarred ones. If you give life, you get life, that was the deal they offered, and so Willie was born. Blonde baby Will, loved then, loved now, and yet the choice (as we must persist in calling it) was tamish. Tamish or downright timid, like all your choices, Locksley. Easy ways out. Finished school and wondering where to live? Come to Boston, they won't bite you there. If you white you all right. Need work? No problem, you already had the one story in *Wyler's*, just go from there. How about a wifie? Already got one! Far out.

So the question why *not* go inside the tavern or 5) on your scorecard is actually an old question. Why not Wyoming or the cold blue Yukon, why not the great grey-green greasy Limpopo River all set about with fever-trees? Why the easy beaten path? True enough that to be an adventurer, to go "on the road" in our time one must also be something of a poseur, mixing myth with folly. Europe choked with wimpy-burgers, Africa a blight of white office-buildings, outer space a dark cold cave full of flying rocks. But isn't there another, harder truth here, namely that adventure resides in the soul, that the domestic nester lacks it there. He is different. He is cozy. (Or "cosy" in Great Britain, where the expression has always enjoyed greater resonance.) He is a valid creature, merely different, and all is well with him so long as he loves "himself". So long as he steers clear of mid-life crisis, for example. For when that happens, he will find out the hard bourgeois truth, he will find there is only the one adventure still open to him, just one within reach—the New Woman Adventure.

Well! Seems we were in for a spot of what we in the trade call the interior monologue (in this case the monologue within the monologue) but it's safely behind us now and I am still hunched at the bar lamenting the narrow tedium of my life, gloryizing the narrow tedium of someone else's. The arm-in-armers at the window table. Tra la, tra la. They are having the double cheeseburg plate, that's y. A dinner fit for dukes and derelicts alike, and they are washing it down with the house rosé, a wine fit for weimaraners, that's y. Because they have no time frame, that *is* why. Little they care the clock is chanting "Go, go, go Locksley go", that it's close onto 6:30 Eastern Standard Time, they don't even hear it. To them it's always just three hairs past a freckle, they are on Freckle Standard Time and even the keenest observer (here I bow low) can have no notion what they do, or why, or where.

I do know that they are acquainted with the three plumbers by the billiard table (very likely a Bourbon-on-the-Charles connection) for they are now passing on the news that a light snow has begun to fall. This flash spreads through the room quickly, like a lighted trail of kerosene, and has an immediate wonderful effect on the total ambience. It is the 19th of December, as I believe I mentioned, but only with this word of snow-fall has it become truly the Christmas season. Magically there are colored lights flickering along the bar, a birch-log fire is blazing away, and carols break out in fits and starts.

The bartender is telling another story, not far from my perch, but this one I cannot hear over the joyful din. A dozen people do hear him, though, and reward him with the rich rumble of laughter. So many undistinguished faces are lit by a smile, transformed as the dullness of zinc is transformed by copper to the bright polished beauty of brass! And now a round of free drinks is cried and the air is literally humid with promise; anything may happen.

I rise.

I am missing Benny's bath. I have forgotten to pick up a pound of butter, though carefully instructed to do so, and I am late for dinner, and hardly hungry for beer-glut, and in less than two hours I will be out in Concord discussing Will and Sadie's problems with Adele. I confess to you I don't even know what Will and Sadie's problems are, reader, discussing them could be tricky. It is, then, four hairs past the freckle, special day or no special day, and I am gone into the night to take a cold slap from the cold snap, in a leave that beery warmth behind and take it on home sort of departure.

It may be worth noting, though, that nothing is all bad. I don't feel bad, for starters, I feel glowy and good and I will not resent Kim or Benny (but oh dear, Kim will resent me) and these spiky little motes of snow pecking at my face are glorious and furthermore I have accomplished something here. I have: taken just a mo and allowed me self to be less dependable upon, played at the jolly freemason. Can a glass of ale en route maison really be the first stop on that thousand-mile glide down to the mouth of the great grey-green greasy Limpopo River where no one is waiting, there is no clock, and 'satiable curtiosity is all one really needs?

Enough. On the march now, around the thinned-out crowds. Down Bridge Street to Fennel Alley, through Fennel Alley to Franklin Avenue, pick 'em up and lay 'em down, on to Locksley Hall.

# LOCKSLEY HALL

Despite its august appellation, you will not find the Hall addressed much as a subject in studies of Boston's architecture. Little has been written of the capital, archetrave and cornice, even less of the cornice returns, on four sides ripped loose by wind and dangling by the last eight-penny cut-nail. Nor has enough been said of the fine neo-crustacean detail of the frieze, so lovingly echoed on the chair-rail and plinth blocks inside. A neglected treasure of early 20th century urban design, this superb four-story walk-up stands as a monument to wood-frame construction. For in an age of cracking concrete slabs and crashing twisted girders where every day is demonstrated the failure of neoteric design and construction, your four-story wood-frame walk-up continues sturdy and serviceable, and shows forth the attention paid to detail and graceful finish on even the lowest class of dwelling sixty years ago.

Locksley Hall! Or 228 Franklin, if you prefer. It is more than just a home, it is affordable. Its shortcomings are few and owe less to structural neglect than to the neglect of absentee landlords. Many of my friends have wondered why I choose to reside here at the Hall, for you have by now fully discerned the partial irony—Locksley Hall is a 3½ room flat of the sort that features "revealed plumbing", not a coldwater flat but lukewarm at times, somewhat beset by rust and grime, a bit of a crush for space if space is what you need, and not really of the best upkeep in regard to plaster or tile.

We sanded and varnished the floors ourselves, as a concession by the author to his bride and by both of us to the age we live in, and I can admit the effect does set Kim's hanging gardens off rather nicely. But the rest is merely a pleasant ruin and I have never been able to explain to anyone's satisfaction why we love it. I never really feel like trying to explain, it seems demeaning to do so. We love it because it is our home, because it is adequate. Because it suits our needs *just barely*, with absolutely nothing of luxury about it, giving us the satisfaction of knowing we are living according to principles embraced at the age of nineteen, or sophomorically.

Why would a man of sufficient means and with a modicum of fame, a man of position, and a woman with means enough herself (for although Kim's poems do not "sell" as such, you might be surprised to learn the number of foundations that these days pride themselves on greasing the palms of Women Who Write)—why would two such people in mens sana reside and even attempt to rear a child in 3.5 grimy rooms four flights above a grimy street, without even the consoling obligatory stink of those two siamese cats whom I must pocket-veto on a biannual basis? Because they like it, that's y.

And that's as far as the explanation ever gets, I'm afraid. It is true that I once lived for two years in a garage with a dirt floor, duck-board and rugs over a dirt floor, and I was extremely, excessively happy there. I may have more to say about my garage life later on this evening but the point is that remarkably little is required to satisfy one's self, much more is required to fulfill the expectations that others place upon our lives, including those who bloody well ought to know better. I and Kim have in common the gift of separating these two matters, and the ability to front essentials. Also it helps that we pass two months each year at her family's farm in Pennsylvania with 58 acres and 14 rooms, 10 fireplaces and 4 rolltop desks. Luxury has made penury easier to bear.

Is there a concern regarding Ben Orenburg Locksley? There is, and yet owing to his youth and smallth it is not a pressing concern. My older son Will, I will wager any sum you care to sign for, is right at this moment (6:42 p.m.) outside in the driveway at his mother's house, and with the spot-lights blazing down from the porch to the clay and gravel rectangle where he conducts the entire National Basketball Association schedule of the Philadelphia 76ers, game by game by game. Sometimes the Sixers will appear in as many as four different games in a given day, Sixers know no fatigue, and likely they will prevail in all four, even when the opposition is the Lakers in L.A. or the Celtics in Boston. Sixers very tough on the road.

He's out there, under the twin spots, playing the part of each performer for each team, shooting the ball in ten different styles and duplicating especially well the individual flair of each man at the foul line. In these games there is realism: the big scorers will score, the rebounders will rebound. Certain coaches will be nailed with a technical, occasionally take a second "T" and get the old heave-ho. But the realism tends to fall away in the fourth quarter. In the fourth quarter the 76ers will always "regroup" and make a charge, the key shots will fall or they will be rebounded (Sixers fierce on the offensive glass when the chips are down) and they will "find a way" to win.

Sometimes I reason that I owe it to Benny to leave his mother and marry Maggie Cornelius, that I incur a sort of obligation to do as much for him in this regard as I have done for his older half-brother. Get him out to the suburbs, get him his driveway by the age of eight, or he'll never have a real shot at the N.B.A. Benny with his big feet could go 6'4" for all we

know, he could be the premier power guard in the league, but
not without a driveway.

Adele thinks Will is sick, of course. That's probably what
tonight's powwow will be about — too much basketball,
too much solitude. She thinks he never got over the divorce,
his game is pure compensation, his loneliness not strong
but sad. (Hope she's wrong. M.L.) The first summer I and
Kim had Will at the farm he fidgeted every second, drove us
batty, till I finally got wise and rigged a hoop on the hickory
tree by the big hay barn. The rest of the summer was as
smooth as glass. He ate, he talked, he swam. He played card
games with Sadie (!), washed the dishes on a volunteer basis,
and fidgeted no more.

Benny will need his driveway — or perhaps he will (they are
individuals, dear) — and if I elect to leave Kim for Maggie he
will have a better shot at it, though I can see Kim balking at
suburban exile. She has always viewed the burbs as a nasty
death, death-in-life, never truly yearned to become Poet
Laureate of Lexington, or Poetess Laureatess of Lincoln or
Leominster. But wait, the schools will frighten her off, you'll
see. Private school is not an option (Kim has her principles)
and the public schools around here will scare the piss right out
of her with all the angel dust and cocaine and sex at twelve or
face a jury of your peers...

It's a mad mad mad world, reader, but I feel safe here at
Locksley Hall, high above the din. Locksley Hall is home, it
has what homes want to have, and Benny says he's happy.
Yesterday as a matter of fact, he said "This is the best day of
my life" for the tenth time this month. Kim thinks he just
heard it somewhere, but I think he means it, each time.

Meanwhile I have entered the hall at Locksley Hall, have
hung my coat on a peg there, and am headed down to the
kitchen to make confession. Kim Orenburg and Ben Orenburg Locksley are both sitting down and I see to my horror

that they have waited dinner for me. Surely it will go the worse for that, the two of them sharp with hunger.

"The butter?" says Kim with a lightly etched grimace. She knows I have forgotten it, she is sure, and I must turn to another sport for my metaphor now: it is a called third strike. I take it right down the middle, drop the bat from my shoulder, and turn toward the dugout. Then suddenly, seeing a chance to at least save face, I turn back to question the umpire's call.

"I thought the boy and I would go fer it together. Like a walk down to Cal's?"

Ben is in his pajamas already and looks up at me like I'm loco. Kim just starts laughing.

"That's awful, Locksley, is it really the best you can come up with?"

"Well, let's see..."

"*Can* I go, Ma?" That's Benny. He has mastered the time-warp and is ready now to maneuver within it.

"Sure," I answer him. "Just yank your trousers on right over your pajamas, and get your shoes and coat."

"Let's just eat," says Kim. "We'll do without the butter at this point. It's seven o'clock, you know."

"But it's snowing. Benny'll love the snow. It's pretty when it's fresh, so white and all."

"Yes, M. We know that."

"*Can* I go, Ma?"

"After we've eaten, boys. You can go fer butter and some dessert, and play in the snow all you like. But you know"—this to me—"you do have a date tonight with A.B. Locksley."

"I do know it."

As we sit down over our stir-fried chicken with onions and green peppers, warmed over lightly, and while I am weeding the onions and the green peppers and the chicken from

Benny's rice for him, I will inject a word or two on the subject of names. It is Kim's habit to call everyone by an initial. Thus Benny is B. and I am M. unless she is gently peeved, in which case I am apt to become "Locksley". My ex-wife Adele is A.B. Locksley, which holds a special irony for Kim in that Adele still keeps my name where Kim herself disdains it. Thus the woman I am married to has not my name, the woman I am not married to has. The rest of the irony is directed toward Adele's weakness for the strong Saxon blend of our joint name: born Adele Blaney, become at age twenty-one Adele Blaney Locksley, she will remain the latter until remarriage sunders her from it, and remarriage will only be assayed with a man of suitably euphonious appellation.

Adele, incidentally, calls me neither M. nor Locksley—to her I am "Reese", she likes that Reese Locksley feeling. To Maggie Cornelius, who has something of a literal bent toward names, I am Maurice, having branded myself forever on the day we met. These labels create expectations, however, and to keep the pressure off just a little, I like to think of myself simply as "Occupant" and I do find that more and more of my mail comes addressed that way.

"How did it go?" Kim asks me, to prove she is not too peeved, thereby inadvertently proving that she is somewhat peeved. She knows I will complain about anything, given half a chance, so this is really a trap, into which I stroll with both eyes open.

"Hopeless," I tell her. "I hate the book."

"You liked it yesterday."

"I did, didn't I? Maybe I like the book but hate writing it. It's just no good me writing in the first person."

"You did say that too, day before yesterday," she agrees, nodding and munching. Ben is unusually quiet, or not unusually; he always beholds in mute amazement whenever I and Kim get started about writing. He listens and gapes but just cannot make any sense of what we are saying. So if he is not now unusually quiet, he must then be "usually" quiet, albeit he is usually not quiet at all!

"Great novels are never written in the first person," I assert.

"So what? You're not writing a great novel. Though it isn't true in any case."

"Citations?"

"Call me Ishmael?"

"Why should I?"

"*Lord Jim, The Great Gatsby*, let me think..."

"Don't trouble yourself. They don't count. The narrator isn't a central character, first person is just a device. You find me one where the protagonist narrates."

"*Great Expectations, Huckleberry Finn*..."

"I said find me one, not two."

"*Catcher in the Rye.*"

"Not great. And all those books are narrated by children. The Russians never wrote in the first person, or the English. Thomas Mann never did it."

"He did so and so did they, and anyway you aren't Thomas Mann."

"Maybe that's the problem."

"You aren't a Russian, either. You're not even English, M."

"You say that and it sounds like I'm not even human, you know."

"We won't go into *that*. Look, why not do something a little different—write your book in the second person."

"Shit, ma'am, I don't even think I could write a sentence in the second person. What the hell *is* the second person?"

"It's how they write advertisements, dear. Like this: You just swung down from the big crane, you're all fucked-up and thirsty as a snake, and now it's Miller Time. So you head on down...etcetera. Get it?"

"Right, right. Second person."

I pour Ben a second glass of milk, Kim and myself a second glass of wine, and I muse about the fact that the second person is precisely the voice one employs to delineate a character who is talking to himself in bars. Like me, for instance, not very long ago. The second person, as it happens, is a resource I have resorted to many times, I just forgot its name.

"Tell me more," I say. "I think I might like to try it in the fourth person."

"Damn that's good, M., I'm just not sure you ought to be changing persons in mid-stream."

"Fifth person, though. Tell me how she reads in the fifth person plural."

"Oh God, enough. Go get the dessert now, willya guys?"

"And the butter!" cries our Benny upon re-entry, for he is far and away the most business-like member of the household. "And play in the snow."

"Good. Let's make a list of these things so we don't forget any of them."

"I won't," he assures me.

"You know, K."—I kid her occasionally too, you see—"I've decided I'm in the wrong line altogether. I've decided to become an electrician."

"What, again?"

"No, the last time it was chimney-sweeping. But I read that all the pretty girls are becoming electricians now. That's the work for me. Wires!"

"You been down in the dark sewer all day long running the big cables, and you're stuck-all-over-shit-and-worms and thirsty as a *bat* and now it's Miller Time..."

Now there are a couple of things that should be said about all this back-and-forth you hear. First of all, I suppose you are thinking, Geez, some pair of garbage-brains these two, eh? And it is true that we live this way, more or less, much of the time, and what's worse we like it. You see, I didn't tell you that lurking beneath the surface of my cosmic discontent, as presented in Bourbon-on-the-Charles, there is this great joy. I can't help it, never been able to help it. Even when I am rock-bottom wretched I am fairly happy, and I can always think of ten or a dozen things I would really love to do, which is the exact opposite of true depression. (Is that a magazine or what, True Depression?) With true depression you can't think up a single blessed thing you even halfway want to do, you're paralyzed, and I know about this because I have had small doses of that paralysis too. Not my fair share, just a taste.

There is more to say, though, in relation to all that verbal silliness I and Kim indulged in at the dinner table. It makes for a small barmy life to be two writers living together, but there are lots of funny possibilities. I don't mean by this Kim's old vision of how it would be if John Updike married Joyce Carol Oates—clack clack clack upstairs, clack clack clack downstairs sort of funny—but rather the way we both get perspective, both see the thing that is happening between us and instantly begin making something else out of it. We can't sustain a fight. Too soon we are parodying the fight itself instead of fighting it, and soon after we are laughing. We even agreed one time to stop at the nastiest moment and each write our own version of how the fray must look to a neutral observer. I laughed at her version, she laughed at mine, and we both changed our minds on the issue; and therefore, unfortunately, had to fight again.

A trifle insular and ingrown to be sure, but then we get on with the business of life too and no one hates us, so far as I know. I'm sure there are worse lives, and there are certainly many strange ways in which the horse-and-carriage of love and marriage rolls along its way. I recall an evening years ago when I was strolling alone near the Boston Common, in a slightly seedy section of Stuart Street, and I noticed a man harassing a woman, tugging at her blouse as she tried to push

him away and move on down the block. He persisted obnox-
iously, clawing at her and drunkenly imploring, while she
calmly and firmly threw off his hands. Finally I arrived to in-
tercede for her, Sir Locksley into the breach!

"Is there any way I can help you, Miss?" I said. And she
laughed uproariously and replied with a single all-
encompassing intelligence,

"Oh, no thank you just the same, he's only my husband."

At which juncture you may be sure Sir Locksley withdrew
precipitously from the joust, while the husband roared in
drunken triumph. He was still lord of his own domain, he had
his rights, and so off they went into a bar-and-grille on the
block to get happy together. That was just one couple getting
on with the business of life, reader, albeit their case makes it
clearer than most why the French call this process l'awful
wedlock!

Now I was making some observations about the banter that
went on at dinner and there is one more to make; we do not
always go on like this, perhaps not even very often. We go on
like this when we are playing our own little brand of
keepaway, when something is slightly out of kilter and we are
trying to make it pass for gaiety. As when Kim is wondering
why I am late by ninety minutes (and why with all those extra
minutes at my disposal I still managed to forget the butter) yet
is damned if she'll confess to such out-and-out pettiness. Or
when I am engaged to visit with Maggie Cornelius later on in
the evening and do not know quite how to arrange my face in
the meantime.

It's easy enough for us and for us, too, quite natural, but it
is all a bit deflected nonetheless, off-course if you will. It
passes but there is a disagreeable distancing in the process that
is felt and not enjoyed, although it can be enjoyed for its own
sake on rare occasions, when the back-and-forth is so much
fun itself that it actually serves to heal the lesion.

So here goes Benny and Pa—yes I am M. and Reese and Maurice and also Pa (to Will and Sadie I was once Pa, am now Dad)—going to the corner variety under a light snow for a few groceries, and as we burst from the foyer into the cold sprinkle of flakes, I see the street is already coated and slippery, and I note with special pleasure that my heart is smiling. You see, to a child the snow must always seem wonderful—there will be no school, there will be sledding instead; snowballs to throw and snow-men to build, hot chocolate and maybe popcorn, too. Whereas for the groan-up the snow has a radically different message, as in Oh groan, the car won't go, the buses won't either, the kids are home from school and fighting. This is a problem, even a tragedy of perception that I am always conscious of, and I try to stay on the right side of the question. I try to peer through the frosted sash and say Oh goody instead of Oh groan and yet sometimes, especially when I remember the accursed automobile, I am heard to groan involuntarily, the sound slips out in spite of all my efforts to youthfully enthuse.

Snow sticking to the ribs of the city. The scene before us is of an absolute whiteness, in the broad glare of the streetlamps even the sky is a swirling cape of white. Street and sidewalk have nearly merged, burying the gutter garbage below, and just now the world is a pristine and magical place. We have five skinny saplings on our block, baby maples granted us by the city years ago, and their knuckly branches are holding the snow, even the pitiful trunks are glazed.

We skip past Ben's favorite window, a place he always wants to visit and therefore has a few times with me in tow. This is the Arcade. The Arcade is one of the many many phenomena in modern life I cannot even begin to fathom. Beyond its tinted plateglass front, some two dozen TV screens are lined up side by side, like urinals, and lined up before them all day every day are two dozen American youths, passionately

Pa and Benny Go Fer Butter

applying body-english to the constant glassed-in collision of
dots and dashes, dabs of light that represent spaceships, dabs of
light that represent bombs. Hundreds of them cram into this
dark chamber to pass the day—the floor is a thick rug of
cigarette stubs, the air is a dense foul carcinogenic fog. A
mouse walking in there would drop dead on the spot from
cancer. To me the joint is as sleazy and depressing as life can
provide, the activity born of total despair, and yet they will
work the games without cease, strung out all day like low-
rent main-line gamblers at the one-arm bandits in Vegas, and
looking every bit as serious in their stake. So much for what I
know about life!

For as I indicated, my own son loves the Arcade. He wants
to live there, if I have understood him correctly, and someday
he may; we all may. At the moment, however, he is able to
keep his mind on the snow, the designated treat, and he at-
tempts to pack a snowball between his palms. The snow is
light dust, the kind that will stick to anything except itself,
and it falls apart through the woolly fingers. I grab his hands
and drag him over the snow fast, right down the middle of
Franklin Avenue, sliding on his shoes, and he laughs wildly
with joy and anxiety. Immediately we stop he is trying to get
a snowball going and once more the elusive powder sifts
through his skinny fingers to the ground.

"Spit on it."

"Yuk!"

"Seriously, kid, drool on it."

"Papa!" he says, working out of his brook-no-nonsense
stance, arms crossed over his little chest.

"Okay, don't. But it won't pack till it's wetter. What was
it we were after—ice cream?"

"Brrrr," says Ben. His shoulder blades are scraping his
earlobes now, he has a posture for every remark.

"Dessert, though. How about pound cake?"

"How about pound cake."

"Right. Pound cake it is. And what else?"

We are at Cal's Variety on the corner and as always Cal is there to wait on us in person. Cal is sixty years old and a few years ago, in great confusion over his failing business, made a few changes which since have made it thrive. He began selling lottery tickets and naked-lady magazines, and of course he cornered, as it were, the tonic and cigarette concession spilling over from the Arcade. Now he's got six thousand a month in new revenue from those sources and all things considered we are lucky he continues to sell us the newspaper and fresh eggs and butter.

"Milk, I think," says Ben. I know he is getting tired, never would have forgotten otherwise.

"That's it! It's butter. The milk reminded me."

"Oh yeah."

I ruffle the thatch of black hair on his head and we settle up with Cal. He hands Ben a lollipop, as usual, and we thank him profusely, as usual. As usual too, I confiscate the lollipop as soon as we round the corner. Cruel cruel.

"Where's your hat?"

Benny shrugs. He has no more idea where his hat is than a dead man would. This kid can lose a hat in broad daylight standing stock still with two groan-ups watching him like hawks. What chance did I have alone in the dark and snow against such sleight-of-head? Another day, another dollar, reader. These hats cost exactly one dollar, you see, I buy them a dozen at a time from the Army-Navy surplus store downtown so that Benny Hatseed here can sow the cityside with them.

"Here, kid, wear mine."

One size fits all! He puts the watch-cap on his head and we start off with our butter and cake. I count off exactly ten strides and then wheel around; the hat is still there. We have less than fifty yards to cover now between here and the Hall, but I have absolutely no illusions about retaining the hat. To me, the hat is already gone. I am thinking about the white snow and Ben's perfect black head of hair. Will and Sadie have lighter hair, Blaney blonde. Ben's is Orenburg black. My own is neutral, mousy brown going on mousy gray. If you ask Ben what color my hair is he'll tell you "no color". Even if you fed him the answer he would say that cause he calls 'em as he sees 'em, like the late Bill Klem.

I am reminded, by blackness and whiteness, of an incident that took place at "school" last week. Benny goes three mornings a week to a day-care where his class is a regular gallimaufry of races and nations. It's even better than an "ethnically aware" place, it's ethnically relaxed, no one is selling anything. There is one boy, however, who is the most race-conscious individual I have ever encountered, much more intensely preoccupied than any adult I've known. The kid, his name is Kabala, does a bit of pounding, the odd fist worked into games and conversations, and last week he stuck a pretty fair left into Ben's bread-basket.

The teacher grabs Kabala and asks him is he sorry. No way. Also if he wishes to spend snack-time on the blue bench in the vestibule. No way. Well if he doesn't tell Ben he's sorry, he will miss snack for sure. (Sorry folks, sometimes you just gotta strong-arm them.) So Kabala turns to Benny and gives him a playful, patronizing sort of fist, friendly fist on the shoulder, and tells him, "Sorry, white."

Can't beat that. Ben scarcely noticed — it was so in keeping with Kabala's character that it sounded perfectly correct. When I joshingly said "Hey white, it's time for bed" that night, he looked altogether perplexed: "Why'd *you* call me white?"

We lie down within the small triangular frontage of Locksley Hall and arc our limbs to make angels in the snow, then start up the stairs brushing off each other's backs. I dart back down to retrieve the hat, catch Ben on the fourth floor landing, and scoop him up in my arms. We are home warm, my pal and I, ready for our cake. Ben and I sit at the table, Kim is already at her desk. I drink coffee with my cake, and bring a cup in to my bride.

"I'm going to grab a quick shower," I say, colloquially.

"Aren't you going to read B's story to him?"

I always read B's bed-time story, it is more or less my purpose in life to do so. It was the main reason I needed Ben, originally, when Will and Sadie were suddenly too old to want me reading to them. The little ingrates wanted to read without me! I learned from the experience, however, and know better now. With those two, reading was encouraged early on, they always had a book in their mitts. With Ben, I encourage TV, dumb puzzles, neurotic eating—anything to hold him back intellectually.

"Of course I'll read, but I want to have a shower first. That way," I conclude brilliantly, "my hair will be dry when I leave the house."

"You don't have to wash your hair."

"I know that, but it just will get wet."

"It *will* get wet after you leave the house too, M. It's just too late. You didn't get home till nearly seven."

"He doesn't have play group tomorrow, though, he could stay up a little longer."

Are we bickering? Are we bickering over nothing, to no purpose? Will we stop soon?

"Choose," says Kim. She has not stopped.

"Shower. Story. Shower."

"Choose!"

"Goodness! I'll read."

I pull Ben into the bathroom and quickly lock the door. I turn on the shower full volume and let it run while Benny brushes his teeth. Kim's feet hurtle down the hall, Kim's hand turns the door-knob.

"Locksley!"

"Just a little joke, puss," I smile, floating the door ajar. "Okay Banjo, let's read."

I yank down a volume of Gogol's short stories and plunge in to the opening of "The Diary of a Madman", waiting for Kim to stop me. Is she baiting me or am I baiting her? Are we having fun? Ben stops me first.

"This sounds dumb."

"Sorry, white."

"Come on, papa. Read Lyle."

I do as much. I find and read *Lyle the Crocodile*, a story which I like but which needs re-writing badly. I generally re-write a story as I read it, except for the handful of great ones, and I know how important it is to record and remember each alteration. If you revise the graven text differently from one week to the next, even slightly, you lose. A kid will call you out on this every time. And when they learn to read a bit over your shoulder, My Lord what a hassle! "You left out that part, papa." (You bet I did, pumpkin, been leaving out the dull parts for years.) "Hey you're right, sweetheart, I did. Good for you." The written word, you see, always the written word, it's sacred.

Now Benny is down for the count and I am standing under the shower feeling okay. Feeling good, actually—good to be home, good to be going out. Perhaps I will stop in for a glass every day at Bourbon-on-the-Charles. Sets you up just right, the workingman's martini, probably sets you up as well each time. But here a hand has entered the shower stall to distract me.

"Ten of eight, you know. You haven't forgotten A.B. Locksley, have you?"

"Memory like an alligator."

"Elephant. Is that why you're getting all spruced up? For Adele?"

"No, Adele likes me a touch grubby. I'm getting spruce for Bruce."

"Well she just phoned to make sure you're coming."

"Did you tell her it's snowing?"

"I gave her credit for knowing, actually. It's just a flurry."

"It could get bad."

"Yes well you'd better not get yourself stuck out there. You make it there, you better make it back."

"We are tough as nails tonight, aren't we? Remind me never to forget the butter again, would you, Tiger Lady?"

"Sorry, M. It isn't the butter, of course. You know. Sometimes it can get to you around five-thirty, six o'clock. Gets you right in the old chemistry."

"Was he cranky?"

"We both were, really. Just a long day's journey into night. You are looking very well, M., by the way. I'll say that much for you."

"That much, eh. Thanks."

"Thanks? Aren't you supposed to go, And you're not so bad yourself, or something?"

Nice to hear we're looking well, reader, and though modesty forbids making any such claim for myself (except to say if you are curious you might check out the dust-jacket photo they used on *Drowning at the Oasis* to get a rough idea) I ought perhaps to provide enough simple data to help form an image before I go on to describe and perhaps even rhapsodize a mite over the Orenburg lass. Myself: an even six feet (sexipede?) and trim enough at 168 but far from feeble, clean-cut shaggy in style with a fair-skinned bony face and killer-gray eyes, and, as noted earlier, the mousy brown hair going mousy gray in spots. None too vivid, I suppose, though I am staring straight at the looking-glass to glean these details. But we were never intended to describe our selves well.

Kim. She is thirty-seven now, looking maybe five years younger. Her eyes are very blue, Caribbean blue, and her curly hair is black. Pretty neat, huh? They are great eyes too, large but quick, sharp and expressive. Her face can be very gay, leaps up allegro, all the features smile. Soft skin never sullied by cosmetics, longish neck, freckles on her breasts (just a few near the top), a swimmer's flat stomach and long slim legs. 5'5", 116 pounds. Favorite eats: Korean beef, when it's done right. Music: the Brandenburg (or sometimes Orenburg) Concertos. Author: George Eliot, whom she tries to remember to call Maryann Evans.

I was about to close out the thumbnail sketch with the topic "Favorite Position", just a half-assed little joke really, and the odd thing is I couldn't prevent a flash image of Maggie Cornelius from cutting in on Kim's portrait. Not because of any peculiarity or exoticism in Maggie's sexual profile; more often than not she'll just climb on, though there is an individuality to it, reader. And one can hardly deny that the sexual aspect looms a bit in a love affair. Anything else is permissible, no one cares about anything else that goes on between a man and a woman, so there is no saying it isn't sex, it has to be sex, hasn't it?

But Kim. I and Kim spent a large part of our first year together in Europe. By the way, I tend to say "I and Kim"—which may strike your ear oddly—instead of "Kim and I" because I discovered early on that I could not say "Kim and I" without envisioning Yul Brynner in *The King and I* and it makes me feel bald just thinking about that play. Hence I and Kim. Hence too I and Maggie, most often, cause now it has become a form of sorts, but not I and Adele cause Adele and I were earlier.

But Kim. And our little trip to Europe. I had been over once before in the role of the mindless tourist, taking the neighborhoods of the continent for so many items on a shopping list, consuming them and checking them off. Kim had been there many times before with the Orenburg entourage—her father is the ambassador—chiefly among what Lyndon Johnson used to call her "fellow Amurricans". We may have had different ideas of what the trip was for, we may have minimized these differences in the planning stage. For me the thing was to break out, to have an adventure—yes, even then. You see I had not gotten around much since Will was born, and then Sadie. I had been grounded in my late twenties, ground down between my family and my literary ambition, and then suddenly I was thirty-three and free. Sort of.

I should have been ecstatically happy. The split with Adele had seemed obvious to us both, a nice harmonious divorce and the kids would be fine. *The 2000 Hour Year* was making headway despite good reviews and I still had most of the advance for *Sweethearts and Criers*, so all was quiet on the fiscal front. Moreover I loved Kim Orenburg, wildly I loved her, could not quench the salty thirst for her, and here we were on the loose together from Stockholm to Paris. There was only one problem. I even knew it. I should have gone on the loose alone that time, I should have done it My Way.

It wasn't so much that I didn't want to see castles and churches and Kim did, that I didn't want to rent cars or sleep in hotels, or eat three square meals a day and call them "breakfast", "lunch", and "dinner", and become upset if food came about some other way. I did have different designs on Europe than Kim but above all, I did not want to be half of a couple. Feeling as I felt about Kim, I may very well have been flat and miserable without her, drifting and killing time; then again, I may not have been anything of the sort. I still had some youth, then, youthful ways of moving into situations. I could have met out of the way people in out of the way places, whole circles of such persons, worlds and underworlds in every city and village—guitars and wine, tobacco and coffee, bedrooms and terraces and small cafés in the cobblestone courtyards behind the shops. All the informal sprawl of life taken on the fly, old myths come to fruition! On the road, the great historical bum, a girl in every port...

And so with half the world starved for affection I had found the most charming lass of them all—sharp without hardness, utterly distracting without a trace of vanity, and funny as Chaplin in a downtown elevator—found her and indeed loved her madly, and yet there I was absolutely drowning in hatred, despising her more every day. Mind, I say all this in retrospect. At the time, we were both pretty damned confused.

We landed up in a cheap hotel room in Paris (not so cheap, actually, but a crummy hotel room in Paris at any rate), our candle burning awfully low and both sick as dogs with Spanish dysentery. In Madrid and Barcelona I somehow kept eating horse-steaks, kept getting them brought to me in varying disguises. The first time it was simply a language problem, I ordered by mis-steak and was just plain saddled with it. After that it was more a matter of pure phenomenology; whatever I ordered, horse-steak came. Deeper and deeper into disease I was driven until finally, by the time we hit Gay Paree, Kim had caught it too and we settled in for quite an unusual stay at the Hôtel Étoile.

As I recall it, we spent a lot of time in the musty corridor pushing and pulling hair in an attempt to get at the bathroom first. The other Étoile patrons were surely nonplussed. They must have been shitting into paper bags in their rooms, or into newspapers like the Yugoslav peasants, because if I ever wasn't in the bathroom, Kim was, and if she wasn't I was. This we had in common, along with the fact that for convenience sake we read the same book that week, *War and Peace*, passing it back and forth in the corridor like a baton. Otherwise there was a distance and animosity to defy every good intention, and to quickly o'ermaster any attempt at decency or tact.

We felt so much better when we finally shook the bug that we actually went out and had fun one night. Saw a good American film with French sub-titles, ate Vietnamese food, and browsed in the teeming bookstalls along the left bank of the Seine. It was not real, though, and it did not last. By bedtime we were at each other's throats again, and after a few more days of the familiar hostility, we concluded it *was* real and might very well last, so we grew decisive.

The plan was this: we would stroll down to the café-tabac on the Rue de Raspail and there we would separate. Kim would pick up a man, I would pick up a woman, and we would see each other next in a week, at our scheduled flight home. This plan we put into operation at once and at once Kim netted her fish, and vanished. But the plan had less to do with ideas of romance than with the exorcism of bile and I soon realized I would need a fresh plan to reflect more accurately what is called in psychiatric parlance "my needs". My new plan was to go straight back to the hotel room alone, read a couple of Simenons and get some sleep; then do whatever I felt like doing, if and when I woke. Pretty smart, right? It is probably true that if you have been beating a head of yours against a wall, merely to stop can make you feel quite at the top of your game, and I did for the hour or so my eyes stayed open. Then around midnight, as I lay peacefully dreaming of autumn nights in America, Kim came back to the room too.

We decided to go home a week early if we could book a flight. We agreed to a six-month separation, after which we would see what if anything was left. We flew out of Paris at lunch-time, were back in the States well before dinner, and

parted after breakfast at the Pine Street Diner, no longer extant. Our six-month separation lasted six days, from Sunday
to the Saturday following, and after that we took the flat
together...

"Benny would like another kiss," says Kim. She is still at
her desk swimming in pages, and the coffee I brought in
earlier stands untouched. Seeing me see it, she remembers
wanting it, and takes it down at room temperature in two
hearty swallows. I duck in, kiss Ben, and return to dress for
my drive to Concord.

"Wish you were coming along?" Kim shrivels at the very
mention of Adele's house.

"I forget the excuse — I mean the occasion. Why is it we're
going again?"

"Will and Sadie's problems."

"Which are?"

"There's only one."

"Really. One problem?"

"No. One 'r'."

"Waste my life, Locksley, go right ahead and waste it. You
never said what kept you till seven."

"It was more like six-thirty."

"Was it anything special?"

"Nope. Yup." Remarkable that she should choose that very
word, le mot juste! *Special*.

"You win, get out of here. I think that this weekend Will
and Sadie and I will get together and discuss *your* problems."

Some pair of garbage-brains, as previously conceded,
though now perhaps you feel the gentle tug of the undertow
too. And just in passing you may find it of interest (I always
have) that Kim does not reduce Will or Sadie to an initial as
she does with the rest of us, they are made an exception. One
thing I do fervently hope, however, is that you haven't taken
a wrong idea of my bride or her disposition tonight. Oh she

may seem a bit aggressive or sarcastic compared to say Ma Kettle, but she really is a sweetie most of the time. Much of what is rough in her comes of battling me, obnoxious Locksley, and when in addition "I" am your historian and sole guide to goings-on, well, keep it in perspective. Check her out sometime on a placid Sunday morning in May, or out among the turnips and potatoes of a Pennsylvania summer, in her cut-offs and kerchief, with Sadie and Ben. She'd melt your heart, reader, take it from Locksley. Did I lie to you in *Selected Essays*?

Even now she has risen to take me in her arms, as though sensing a bad press. "If you get home early enough," she says, "you might find that not *all* the pretty girls are becoming electricians."

Very few, I'm sure. I can appreciate the generosity of impulse behind this uncharacteristically kittenish overture and still I am forced to scramble a bit in the circumstances. "Tricia!" is what I say, God knows why, my muse gone balmy, for though I have a thought in my head it is a thought of Maggie Cornelius who will be waiting for me after my chat with Adele and who will through no fault of her own insure that I am home anything but early.

"Tricia the Electrician!" I go on, staggering but clutching the ball. "A boffo spot, K. Have some cards printed up at once. 'Nothing fishy when Tricia fishes your wires, sires. You'll wish you had Trish, what a dish...'"

"M., you turkey."

"Won't fly?"

"Maybe in the 5th Grade it will. You'd better hit the road before you short out."

"Is the car still in Fennel Alley?"

"I doubt it's moving, if that's the punch line."

"Maybe it's been stolen. Maybe it won't start. See you. And don't forget to water the Rizzi."

"I already watered all the paintings today, don't worry so."

I have kissed the crown of her head and am again winding down the four flights of familiar stair to Franklin Avenue. Sometimes at this hour, expecially after too rich a dinner or too much ale, I get logy and useless for about an hour, but tonight I am fresh and spilling over energy. Does this strike you as an indication of less than pluperfect stability? Where I tell you one minute of my crushed spirit, my nagging displeasure, only to turn around and next minute say I feel like a million quid? A trifle schitzy? Well that's me, darlin'!

May be it was those two ale, or possibly the bright young snow. May be it's the special calibre of the day, not the day which began last mid-night or this morning at cock-crow but the one which began at 5:00 p.m. outside Bourbon-on-the-Charles, the day I decided to share with you in detail. May be it's being glad to see the kids, and Adele, and Maggie C. We'll C.

## MARVINS AND MELVINS

The Boston area is intriguing from the sky at night, as any coastal city is. There are the strings of light, bridges and passes, the rings of light on the island beltways, clusters of light in the parks and squares. The fainter grid of light gives way to a gradual dimming as you drift inland, till by the time you are over the distant suburbs there is a remarkable ratio of dark to light, of treeland and grassland to crushed land and macadam.

The progression is also seen in the various efforts to purvey modern housing along the route. Your initial brush with the alarming notion "If you lived here you'd be home now" comes virtually in the shadow of the airport where for $65,500 (and that's 65-5 in the parlance) you are offered two rug-over-concrete rooms with a pinch-window view of three major beltways snarled below a cloverleaf—the graying of America!

The truth is, if you lived here you'd cut your throat tout de suite, mon ami, but things do get better as you head west and soon enough you are offered for 75-5 a four room row-house condo with a parking slot, a patch of grass, and an airtight wood-burning stove "imported from Europe". (How else would it get here, really?) If you lived here you'd be home now too, and yet would you *feel* at home?

If not, simply roll down the window, punch in the radio, and continue west until you eventually do bear down on a bonafide suburb—Girl Scout cookie and Little League baseball sort of suburb—where you will buy for 115-5 a "home" (not a "house"), fill the garage with 12-speed bicycles, and barbecue off the deck in back. There will be a mall nearby to meet your several shopping needs and to keep the wolf of isolation from yr dr (have to watch this realty-speak, it realty stays with you) and you will be truly home now, back in the U.S.S.A.

Adele does better still, of course, on Blackberry Lane in historic Concord, where late the embattled farmers stood and frd the sht hrd rnd the wrld. For one thing she tapped into the Locksley millions at the time of the move—we went for a settlement based on paperback royalties from the Wockenfuss Trilogy—and then for the last five years she has been turning a buck herself as owner-operator of Locksley Arts and Crafts, distributing art supplies to the school systems of some of the richer towns out this way. If you have ever wondered where the mark-ups were, reader, then wonder no more. Oil would be a poor guess, so would gold bar or crunchy granola. Art supplies to the gifted brat, that's where the mark-ups are, I won't even name a percentage. Adele did not create the situation, she merely stumbled across it and leapt to take advantage. In truth she got the accounts by proffering a better line at a lower price than the older companies, and still I won't name a percentage.

Had we been making the move to Concord together, Adele has frequently said, she would have been leaning toward an elegant house from an earlier period, with kempt extensive grounds and charming outbuildings, immense old deciduous shade-trees and a small orchard on the hill, set back from the twisting road by a few well-spaced cedars and the hand-fashioned loose-rock wall. Since the idea of moving to Concord came subsequent to the idea of divorce, however, we were not going to Concord together, and so she bought instead the new seven-room house on Blackberry Lane, sometimes known as "Locksley West."

I have heard it said the pot shouldn't presume to call the kettle black so I will describe briefly and without prejudice the housing development on Blackberry Lane. Or rather the development named Blackberry Lane, since the road itself came as part of the package. There was no such lane before they drained the swamp. Bushmill Road was there a long time to judge from the modest landed estates along it, but the 60-acre swamp had never been anything more than a skating pond before the drainage. They put the road through and raised thirty houses over the fill, and the houses were okay. They used good materials and did extensive planting so that each 2-acre lot would look different from the next and the prior. And they unloaded all thirty with no difficulty at all despite the price.

But the swamp still haunts those thirty houses on Blackberry Lane. Haunts them especially in winter when massive, glacial frost-heaves muscle the foundations, re-arranging anew each year the many ways in which the various doors and windows malfunction. Then in April and again in August the thirty basements fill up with water, from one to four feet high. Many are the tales of the heroic Marvins and Melvins who strip to the buff and swim those murky cellar waters in quest of floating pets, small appliances, and sundry other valued jetsam.

Those Marvins and Melvins do not swim the cellar of Adele Blaney Locksley, though they would eagerly do so if asked. I am asked, generally, and I have swum, though mostly I drink Adele's fancy coffee and argue with her about selling the house. She's happy at West, though. She likes it, likes her job—enjoys being "out there" is how she puts it, out in the world after all those years of seeing only children and their hamsters. It was a little, she once said, like learning to walk again after a long convalescence.

She has a pretty good man too, I've met him a number of times and can't say a bad word about him. Oh maybe one: Bob Berger is *too* nice. He is so nice he cannot be forceful. If I barged in on them in bed and ordered him out of the house, I'm pretty sure he'd go. Jump up, dress nervously, and depart, saying "Yes yes it's true, you knew her first..." He is a guy so dedicated to letting it all run smoothly that for smoothness' sake he will bear any indignity. You could smother him with a fart and he wouldn't bat an eye or make a move, not even shade away on the sly. I'm talking about a bone-crushing fart here, reader, of the sort that might level any other mortal and old Berger will forge bravely past to the next topic of conversation.

Merely good manners, you may say, and of course you could argue it that way. But I have a feeling Adele can't love him. She will try, for she knows his points and she knows one can't have everything. Often she has noted that he's a deal better to her than I could ever have been and that's so, it's all too obvious. And still I fear she can't love him, though he worships the wall-to-wall she walks on.

Will's fond of him, though, and I'm proud of the lad for that. Berger doesn't know a basketball from a cowsquash and for Will that makes the man a conversational zero. But Will loves Berger, he protects the guy's feelings all the time in little ways, tries to make him feel right at home out there at Locksley West. Will's a good one, all right, he'd bring tea and toast to a cloth monkey. First time he met Kim he was only seven. I could see he really took to her and that he just wasn't sure if it was *okay* to like her. He asked his mother that night and she told him, if you like her you like her, so Will gets on the phone straightaway to let Kim know he likes her. Tells her he forgot to say it before but that he really does. Kim cried hideous tears that night, reader, touched by my son's sincerity, as I was too.

But Berger will have his troubles with Sadie. I haven't said
too much about Sadie thus far and I may never because she is
in many ways a mystery to me. Also because she is so strong
and independent. Two years younger than Willie, she seems
almost free-standing, like a sculpture, tough as pig-iron. So I
really don't worry about her a lot and though we have always
been close in the past, just this year she seems more inward or
peerward or something—just-got-my-first-bra, nothing-left-
to-say-to-pa sort of daughter maybe—and I have resolved to
wait her out. I know we'll be great pals when she comes out
the other side, in her twenties.

Sadie all but spits at that guy Berger though, as I say, lately
she looks like she'd as soon spit at me too. All this spitting!
But wait, Sadie hasn't actually spat at anyone yet, it's just a
face she puts on now and again. I can see Berger doesn't know
what to make of it, or how to handle it, and I have also seen
Will try to guide him past it, nursing Berger along with
polite questions about his work (I believe he teaches history)
and in somewhat a reversal of their expected roles bracing up,
as it were, Berger's incumbency.

The bland suburban life is not as much of a comedown for
Adele as you might suppose. We never lived the life of celebri-
ty at all, never went to parties or promotions or to the colony
of Hollywood where the swells like to take a Creative Person
to lunch. It was business as usual for us, not life in the fast
lane but life in the breakdown lane, laundromats and pizza and
cars that had to go black-market for an inspection sticker. We
lived a bland suburban life in the city, in which I came home
from work at 5 p.m. as I do now. Like everyone else, we took
an occasional trip but for the most part we stayed home and
raised the kids.

Over the years I was unfaithful to Adele only once, or with
only one woman, the redoubtable Karen Comiskey. Like the
Venus de Milo, K.C. had no arms, literally. But to go along

with this affliction, she had been provided with a most
dramatically female body, such round firm thises and thats,
and only God can say why it amused him to clip her wings.
Of course I do not do pornography, even in the leanest years I
wouldn't touch it, and yet K.C. always struck me as the
perfect gimmick around which one might build such a book;
plus ça change, plus c'est la même chose sort of porno, you
know.

When I met Karen she told me she restored antique furniture, that's how she worded it exactly. This was her test for
me and I passed, by gaping at her. Bob Berger would have
nodded and smiled, packed his pipe and maybe faintly red-
dened in spite of himself, but I gaped and stared down at the
places where her arms weren't and she accepted me, she let me
inside her world. "I've always enjoyed working with my
hands," she said, a line I resorted to myself early in this account and no doubt to less effect. It was another test and I
passed again, by laughing, though I shook my head in amazement too, for this was brass with a capital b (so make that
Brass), this was one tough lady and I was very much taken
with her.

She *was* in antique restoration by the way, had a little place
on the North Shore and chased around after lower-case brass
and birds-eye maple to buy. Not that she couldn't have done
more. I know of one man at least who paints wonderfully
detailed landscapes with the brushes held between his teeth, as
he too has no arms. Locksley's Believe It or Not! (Believe it,
it's true.) At any rate, I was soon out there with her in hot
pursuit of dry-sinks and high-boys, as even sooner we had
fallen in sex, which is like having fallen in love at first but not
two months later. There was nothing strange in it, nor
anything terribly strained. K.C. was a compensator and like
the blind seer of classical irony, she saw to it that her delivery
was undiminished by her affliction.

Her sense of humor was not at all forced, it grew from her misfortune like a native plant. She was always joking about the Cripple Rights Amendment, and Crip Lib—her shorthand of course for the Liberation of the Disabled—and she had a whole skit worked up about getting out the Cripple vote at election time, for who would be most sensitive to the crippling aspects of life, both physical and metaphysical, and who would install the ramps and rollways to a whole life for every citizen? I loved her toughness, her humor was real, and still I did find the situation had warped her. There was this *slight* warp and with it came a foreboding about the future, the following-through.

This is a phenomenon I have noticed and which I was in fact reminded of again only yesterday at the Dim-Sum Fast-Treat, Kim's favorite Szechuan take-out. While I waited idly for our spring rolls, bawdz, and beef w. water chestnuts to emerge, I glimpsed for the first time in eight years a fellow named Alex Pickleman. Pickleman used to play on the same softball team as I back then, and drink a little beer during and after the games. We were friendly enough on that level. Seeing him yesterday after so much time was a shock, not because of the ways he had changed; quite the opposite, he was precisely the same. He told all the same jokes with all the same inflections, was working the same job for all the same reasons, and looked so much the same he might have been his own brother! I thought at first he had not even cut his hair, or grown it, whereas in fact of course he had cut it a hundred times simply to maintain stasis.

Poor fucking Pickleman! I made him the occasion for pity, but it really was self-pity in pitifully thin disguise, for to me he revealed anew how very little we change from the cradle to the grave, how solidly we are our selves at the age of six months (if not six minutes) and remain steadfastly our selves to the end. This is the business of following-through to which

I alluded, the way in which we once take shape and make our choices, and then must live out those lives on the conveyor-belt of character we've built, all according to the outline. You are what you are, reader, it's a belt comes round. You live the *rest* of the life you have once begun.

For Karen Comiskey the following-through contained this small ineluctable warp. And felt inexplicably bleak to me in consequence. This chapter in my life was neither a charity on my part nor any kind of kinky thrill-seeking, and it was not an episode of humanity research, either, by that old humanist and sometime novelist Locksley. It was a love affair, was what it was, which concluded, as most of them do, in ways that escape the memory...

But Adele. We were discussing Adele. She never learned about Karen (even as a rookie husband I was slick with an omission) yet they remain connected not only in the obvious way but also through a rather odd association, with sculpture. I never cared for statues myself, though I concede the great ones are a power in the flesh (or the non-flesh, I suppose), and I don't know that K.C. liked them either. She simply could not avoid the Venus de Milo riff, she would even get it from drunks on the subway platform. So she rolled with it and deadpanned that her fortune would be made if they ever did a movie version of the Venus, or even a remake of the statue.

Whereas Adele by chance actually *was* once emblazoned in bronze, albeit with both arms raised behind her head. Nowhere in Adele Blaney's body has anyone ever found an artistic bone, yet the bones themselves were always sound enough and when she ran with Barney Waters, the sculptor, she inevitably sat for him too, as they were young. I met Barney later, having overlapped with him slightly, and once over whiskeys we jested about Adele's penchant for martyring herself to men of artistic pretension.

Barney made it in Manhattan, God love him, and in the
process conferred upon Adele the permanence of Art, as Lotte
Buff was apotheosized by young Goethe, or perhaps with a
touch less grandeur. But a figurine begotten out of Adele by
Barney was snapped up by the Rockefellers, though I cannot
say which branch, and so was born the family joke; that
whatever came my way, even should I one day be awarded the
Nobel Prize (in what field, you may ask facetiously, but re-
read *Sweethearts and Criers*, re-reader, there's more there than
meets the I) Adele would still have achieved immortality first,
the day her ex-boyfriend sold her body to the Rockefellers.

Of course Adele has "followed through" herself, even in the
wake of her immortality. Kind of odd to see her now, the almost fulsome businesswoman in tweeds, and to recall the lithe
and casual (if slightly political) nudity of her youth, as cap-
tured in the famous figurine. Lovely conjunction of underarm
and breast, hip muscle high and shining and wonderfully
enlivened by a minutely subtle twist of the upper torso, and
then the completely featureless face. Not even a hint of nasal
protrusion, nothing in fact but the clay smoothed over. Certain critics were blown away by the significance of this "statement", as were the Rockefellers I suppose, branches
notwithstanding.

Even Adele knew the truth; that Barney Waters had long
enjoyed an obsession with the large central portion of a
woman, from the neck to roughly the knees, and that he was
totally and admittedly inept at doing "heads". ("Heads" being
the sculptor's terminology for, well, heads.) He could not do
them because he lacked all interest, he lacked all interest
because he could not do them. Whichever. The Rockies were
made happy and that's always the vital thing.

## AXE IN SPACE

assing up at the wood-frame Sunoco less than two minutes from Blackberry Lane. I always step out of the car when I buy gasoline, we all will soon enough when there's no one else to pump it, but I like to get out and stretch, to sample the air.

It's a class thing partly, or an anti-class thing, disliking the feeling that someone is waiting on me even if he happens to be bleeding me for the service. Also I despise any confinement, including automotive, so there's always a relief to climbing out of that naugahyde gondola into the wide open spaces. It's a lot like the sensation I had as a boy, whenever they made me wear a tie around my neck and finally I was allowed to rip it off and breathe again. Good God, reader, do you wear a tie around your neck, are you wearing one now? For gosh sakes, why?

"That's fourteen even, sir."

The voice belongs to a spare well-groomed lad of sixteen in a green jump-suit. The mechanic has long since gone home, and the hangers-on, so this youngster is left alone with the money, at the mercy of any means, and instinctively I wonder if I would allow this for Will.

"Thank you very much," I say.

"Thank *you*, sir."

"Maybe if you're lucky there won't be any more customers tonight. Warm in there?"

"Oh yeah. No problem. You get too hot in there after a while. It's kind of nice coming out to the pumps."

"Well, take care now."

"Thank you, sir."

Nice boy, just a trifle too well brought up, that's all. But now as I dive back into my naugahyde confinement I can hear Sadie's favorite admonishment ringing in my ears, for I have projected Will into a situation, and weighed it for him, so why not for her? "That's *sexist*, Dad." I guess it is!

I pumped gas as a kid, my first honest buck and all, and there was certainly no way a girl could get those jobs back then. Or want them. What about that, Sadie? You want equality at the top, not at the bottom, there's plenty of *lousy* jobs for everyone, what you want is decent jobs. What's that you say, you want free choice, top and bottom being a matter for individual determination? I really have to learn how to beat Sadie to the punch, that's the thing. An opening at the Getty station in Littleton, manning as it were the pumps. Suggest it to her and when she blanches involuntarily, let her have it quick with both barrels: "That's *sexist*, Sadie."

On your left now the Bensons, who got three fir and one maple; on your right the Kransteins, three maple, one fir. Remember? Locksley's Sociology of Homes! I swing into Adele's driveway, 11 Blackberry Lane under my surname on the galvanized mailbox, and roll to a halt well back from the horse-shoe turnaround because the game is on and the game is serious business. The snow is falling more heavily out here. It has settled on the soft needles of the big scotch pine and glistens among the tiny Christmas lights the kids have strung up and lit. The storm has blotted out any sign of the nearest neighbors, and has thereby rendered Adele's house the more inviting. There's a kindling glow in the gable window and above Will's dormer the thickly rising smoke from the brick chimney mingles with the swirling snow. The aroma of applewood is somehow clear down here in the driveway, a sensation which I must question aerodynamically, since smoke rises, is visibly rising. Can A.B. Locksley have put on a special effects crew for the evening performance?

Will is apprised of the weather, for he has recently done some shoveling in the area under the basket, but he is undeterred. I see his dim figure flashing to the basket, scooping the ball up through the tumbling snow to the floodlit goal. Back out to the top of the key, down into the low post, wheeling to the baseline—in! Will must have seen me coming, or heard the gasp of my aging engine, but he does not slow or stop, and I know he will not. He "has his concentration" you see, and is performing obliviously before 15,000 hoarse fans in the Garden. Not Eden, but any other Garden, Omni, Mecca, Spectrum or Palestra, paradise all the same. His shot hits back iron but Will grabs the rebound (who else?) and takes it in for the unmolested lay-up. And he's right back in the lane with a great steal, drops the easy jumper.

"Hey, you're hogging the ball."

He has tremendous court vision, my boy Will. He knows exactly where I am without looking and the pass whips into me in the half-dark at the edge of the penumbra even before I have finished accusing him. I find the handle on the ball, though it is wet and cold, and run a bounce pass back to Willie underneath. Two!

"You shoot it, Dad," he says, lobbing the ball right back out to me. Bang! "Wow, I didn't think you could hit from way out there."

"That shot is like a lay-up to me, Willie-boy."

"Take another."

"Tell me how you are first, you wild-eyed fanatic. Did you notice it's snowing?"

"Duh now."

"Duh now? Do they still say that?"

WILL AT WEST

"Apparently," he replies, to prove he can go both ways with his sarcasm as well as his basketball.

"That's better. The cool rapier-like wit. Let's see how you shoot the jumper lefty."

"Lefty?"

"Sure."

"Come on, Dad. You can't shoot lefty."

"The hell you say."

I'm still holding the ball but I have stolen forward into the lane, just ten feet away from the basket. I bounce the ball once for rhythm and pop in a left-handed jumper, or toe-launch pseudo-jumper. The bald luck of it! Now my son will respect me all week, because I had the hot hand Tuesday night at Locksley West.

"I've got to go in and talk with yo muthuh," I say, by way of returning his pass.

"She's not home."

"What? I just drove all the way out here in a snowstorm at her behest and she isn't home?"

"Well maybe she's home. I guess she is."

Now I am really buffaloed. What can be the meaning of this soft-headedness? Is there such a thing as reality here at West? My son the franchise, he does it all at both ends of the court, he "sees the whole floor" but does he see nothing else? Is Adele right about this?

"Is your sister home?" I try him out.

"She'll be home any minute, Dad. She's across the street sitting for the Gerber Baby."

"Who for?"

"The Gerber's kid. She calls it the Gerber Baby—you know —but I think it's really about eight years old."

"It?" I ask, another intended check, but this time there is no response forthcoming. By Will's lights I have already been given a generous amount of time. He has halted the game and left 15,000 hoarse fans sitting on their hands for my sake and now enough is enough. Top of the key, in the lane, the quick cross-over dribble and up (with the left hand!)...rolls off the rim, rebound to Will (who else?), he sco-o-ores!

The snow is half a foot deep on the front walk and on the terrace, drifted in over the rhododendron and the bare forsythia stalks. Berger's little vegetable garden is under so much hay and snow that it now looks like there are bodies hidden in the yard. I rap on the sliding glass door, as I always do, so that Adele will part the heavy drapes and motion me around to the side entry. The slider has never worked and can never be made to work, so far as I can tell, but I like to go through this charade out of the mildest perversity and feeblest humor. It is so stupid of me to persist in this moralizing that even Adele finds it an amusement by now.

"I'm glad to see you're home."

"Of course I'm home. What made you think I wouldn't be? You're late."

Adele is dressed in an ankle-length baby-blue sweatshirt, complete with hood. Normally I despise any piece of clothing that looks as though someone just thought it up last month, but I admit to myself that this job appears both comfortable and fetching. I can tell by her smug unspoken pleasure that Adele reckoned beforehand I would like it in spite of my godawful principles. She believes I deplore too many things, has often wished I would get some other *kind* of principles. But we know each other pretty well, Adele and I, and can afford to skip a great deal without necessarily missing any.

"I didn't say I thought you wouldn't be home. I said I am glad to see you are," I reply, unwilling to incriminate my vague-headed son despite the initial slip.

"So how are you, Reese?"

"I'm well enough," I respond meaninglessly. "You look fine."

This is the truth. Adele knows me, as I say, knows I might just as well have said "You look like hell" and so absorbs the remark with unintentional pleasure, as all of us absorb any flattery. Adele always looks comely in soft pale things, blue and yellow. When I see her at her best I have trouble believing she can be the parent of two teen-aged children. And then to think that I am too—the same two children!—it boggles this boysenberry's brain. I can never decide if it makes me feel younger or older, this seeming anomaly, this shock of recognition, though I can assure you it makes me feel very strange.

"Like some coffee?"

"If there's no beer."

"There is beer, if you'd rather. I'll split one with you."

"Let's split two."

"The usual way?" she grins.

I shrug yes. The usual way, of course, is half a beer for her, 1½ for me. It's not that I'm greedy, mind you, just that she wants one half and I want 1½. Why knock it? It's worked for years and politics isn't all that much fun anyhow.

In the living-room I examine the mechanism of the sliding glass door and tug at it futilely with a shake of the head. This too is ritual. Now we take up our stations, Adele on the sofa and I in the overstuffed, get our legs and feet arranged, and Adele completes the preliminaries by asking after Benny.

"He's good. But I hope you know he's planning to move in with Will. He wants to."

"God knows what for. You know what time Will got started out there tonight?"

"Five o'clock?"

"I'll give you a hint. He didn't come straight home after basketball practice. I had him pick up a few things at Walter Jordan's store."

"Thanks for the clue. Five-thirty."

"Correct. And did he stop for dinner?"

"Yes and no. He stopped, because you insisted, but he ate all his food in less time than it takes to say Grace, fidgeted unbearably for thirty seconds more, and then sprinted back outside as soon as you couldn't bear the fidgeting any longer."

"You sound so glib about it, Reese. It is a serious problem, you know."

"Is it? Is it the subject of tonight's meeting?"

"You sound glib about everything, don't you? Don't you care about you son's life anymore?"

"Oh come on Dell, please. Tell me. What did he get at Jordan's store—was it pound cake and butter?"

"You're a genius. How did you ever guess?"

"I'm a genius," I shrug by way of explanation, even as her fingers grasp the fringe of the rug to yank it out from under me.

"Well, he got five pounds of potatoes, a string of onions, half a pound of hamburg, and some wax baggies. Is what he got."

"Ah." I polish off the ½ and pick up the 1. "Tell us then luv, what *is* tonight's topic?"

"Please don't be frivolous," she implores me, tilting her head prettily and with a winning frown. How can I explain? I *sound* frivolous, but God how I care. Doesn't Adele know this much about me? I am utilizing every ounce of strength in my upper body right now to keep from tilting *my* head and frowning back. Satire is too strong a vein in me, it has gone out of control.

"Tell me, then."

"It's not just Will. It's Sadie too."

"What is 'it' though? Surely Sadie my little lady has not been out shooting baskets in the snow past midnight."

"I wish she had. I'm afraid your daughter has other games in mind."

"What? What's she done?"

"Well she's gone out several times with Mike Palmieri, who happens to be older than Will. And she wants to go out with him both nights this weekend. I think this is going to be 'serious' before we know it, and I'm not at all sure I can deal with it."

"Are you sure you'd mind so much if it was Bobby Webber she wanted to go out with? Maybe this is just your old anti-Italian prejudice rearing its ugly head."

"Reese, you shit. How dare you say that! Why would you think I was prejudiced against Italians?"

"Because you are?"

"In Italy, you mean. And those stories were simply *true*. This is just a nice American kid with an Italian name."

"Oh. What's in a name, then? But if he's such a nice kid, why so worried? You know, Dell, there is definitely something very decent in the Italian male character, because when I was a kid my two best pals were Italian boys. They were incredibly sweet human beings."

"In that case I'm surprised you liked them! The point, Reese, is that Sadie is twelve years old. If you can get all this ethnic stuff out of your head long enough to look at that one fact squarely. She's twelve and she may be about to announce she is 'going steady' with Harry Handsome from the highschool, who is probably fifteen or God knows sixteen, and the next thing you know she'll be asking to get fitted for a diaphragm."

Adele reaches me with this one. I exhale, and admit to myself it is disturbing and what's worse, I haven't the foggiest notion how to react to it.

"And Will?" I say.

"Okay. Sadie is twelve and she is interested, to put it mildly, in boys. Will is fourteen and he's no more interested in girls than... I don't know, Reese, you supply the metaphor."

"Than Richard Nixon is interested in Truth. How's that sound? It would be nice to know we still have Richard Nixon to kick around after all!"

"The hell with you."

"Wait a mo, Dell. It's just I'm not sure we have such a tough problem here."

"Oh? What's the answer?"

"Don't worry?"

"And why not?"

"Well, let's see. Because it's normal?"

"Which?"

"Both?"

"Sadie has her period, you know. She could become a mother this weekend."

"Overnight? The hell with gestation! But that's a biological reality, Dell, not an emotional problem. There's certainly nothing we can do about the biology. We can't have her spayed, you know. And really, aren't girls supposed to get silly about all this earlier on than boys? Don't you trust her?"

"It just isn't that simple. Of course I trust her. I do. But it isn't easy facing the demands of the highschool hero in the back seat of a car, it can be very confusing. You can forget what you know."

"They always remembered with me, I'll tell you. But seriously, and I am as serious as can be about this, believe me, there's nothing for it but to trust her and keep the lines open. And I think it's fine to limit her to one night a weekend and nothing on school nights. I'll take the weight on that one, if you want."

"That's nice, but you aren't here to take the weight when it actually comes up. It isn't like that anyway, you know, you don't simply tell a kid her age the Rules as though that's all that needs saying. They question you and wheedle and sulk and try to push you around."

"I'm not in school with her either, but I tell her how to behave there. So do you. So let's not get into the I'm not here part of it, cause that's a sidetrack from way back."

"Okay, but it is part of the problem. I didn't say you *ought* to be here, only that you aren't. A mere fact?"

"I'll talk with Sadie before I leave. I can't say more without a better feeling for what she's thinking."

"Good. Try. It isn't easy talking. And I hope you'll try talking to Will too, while you're at it."

"What for, though? Talk him into taking an interest in girls? I feel we should leave him be. When he's ready for girls there'll still be a few around. He's okay, you know."

"He isn't."

"Kid's out there learning a trade, he's off the street, keeps his nose clean. Why look for problems where they don't exist?"

"I'm being overly dramatic. That's what you think? Is that the opinion of L.F. Orenburg?"

The initials stand for Laissez-Faire, Dell's little jest on Kim, whom she can't help disliking at least slightly. The use of the letters you understand already; the rest of the jest pertains to Kim's philosophy of child-rearing and life in general, basically that it's all decided, we are just helpless insects in the lap of the Cosmos and it is a waste of strength to discuss discuss discuss unless the discussion starts to get funny. (See her wonderful long poem "Axe in Space" if you want these ideas with the force of her own words behind them.) Adele on the other hand loves to discuss, even independent of clarity or the hope of progress, God forbid truth. She likes the *process* of discussion, socially.

"No, not very dramatic at all, actually," I say, leaving Kim out of it, which is only as it should be. "But you do delve into things this way, analyzing emotions, and I think sometimes you forget..."

"I forget what?"

"I don't know, I lost track of what I was saying. I'll talk with Sadie, because there is something to talk about. But I can't get into it with Willie, because there isn't anything to say. It'd be like asking Berger why he doesn't like basketball, why he isn't interested. He just isn't, that's all."

"It's quite different."

"Of course. But it's almost analagous."

"I don't think so, Reese."

"Look, thank your stars and drop it. As far as I can tell, it would work out best if the kids both got interested in the opposite sex around sixteen, did a little dancing, stayed away from real sex till at least seventeen, and then used their intelligence and discretion."

"Aren't you the dreamer."

"Yes but why not be grateful that Will, at least, is on that schedule? Just because Sadie isn't? Count your blessings."

"Reese, the counselor at school thinks Will is a bit imbalanced in his interests."

"He is that, obviously. But he has all A's on his report card."

"True."

"True? You said, 'True'?"

"Well yes, it is true."

"I know that, but we were arguing. We were disagreeing and you stopped, and heard what I said, and said in reply, 'True'. That's so extraordinary. It's wonderful."

"Mister Glib is back, I see. You are hopeless, Reese, do you know that? There's only one thing you're good for."

"What a cheap shot."

"It was meant as a compliment, actually."

"What a shoddy value system."

"You don't want to go to bed?"

"Bed!"

Adele is not serious, reader, she knows as well as you or I that Will may pop in at any moment for a slug of root-beer or Ovaltine at one of his numerous half-times, that Sadie too is expected momentarily and for all I know maybe Berger into the bargain.

"We haven't been to bed together since 1976, you know."

Of course I know. Such a wooden, rhetorical remark. But what can she be driving at?

"Do you remember the Bicentennial Fuck?" she says, keeping right after it.

"Was this in celebration of the 200th anniversary of Fucking?" I reply disingenuously, impersonally.

"Independence," she says, "as declared. By Thomas Jefferson and Adele Blaney Locksley."

"*Those* two. They could really boogie, those two. But you were independent years before that," I remind her.

"Not really, though. Do you remember?"

"Of course I remember. Kim gave me hell for over a year because of the Bicentennial Fuck." She still gives me hell about it, reader, but best not to let Adele in on that. A home-shot might really get her going.

"Why don't we have one now, Reese. C'mon, just a quickie."

She's being cute with it, she is not serious. May be she is casting for a compliment. May be that explains it.

"You do look fit, I'll say that. But let's let sleeping dogs lie. Ever onward sort of thinking, you know."

"Just a quickie."

Adele is close to me now and smiling, there are certain distinct impressions of her pushing against the soft blue flannel, indeed there is evidence of her apparent sincerity in the air itself.

"You know what Dylan Thomas said about his poems? He said, if he didn't just leave them well enough alone they would never be finished, he'd never finish a one of them."

"Don't quote alcoholic poets at me, just get your pants off."

She is smiling differently now, however, the crude act she can't quite bring off smoothly. But she's saved by the belle, as Sadie Locksley, age 12½ (and allegedly armed with sanitary napkins in among the chewing-gum wrappers and bitten pencils in her book-bag) enters and exits the room in one smooth motion, dashing right past us up the stairs.

"Your father is here," Adele calls after her, fully composed.

"Hi Dad!" she calls back. "Right with ya."

"I was just testing your resolve, Reese. You did very well."

"Very strong my resolve."

"That must be nice for you."

"Listen, Dell. The truth is I don't want to fuck. I don't even want to talk. I want to go out and play in the snow. I don't want to be a 40-year-old father agonizing over the hazards of teen sex, I want to sprint out over the snow and roll around, toss up a few shots, ice-skate by lantern light at Walden Pond..."

"Don't let *me* stop you," she laughs uncomfortably. She is clearly affronted in some nameless way yet can find no real complaint to make save to identify me as an immaculate fool.

"I want to talk with Sadie, remember?"

"I thought you wanted to go play in the snow. Poor confused little boy, wants so many things."

"That was a statement, Adele, a sort of prose-poem. You took it much too literally."

"Stupid of me. Not really up to the mark, am I?"

Merry Christmas! You better talk to her, reader, she is beginning to get to me and I will need all my energy to attack Sadie's situation with the correct patience and loving tact.

(Yes I agree that 'loving tact' is perhaps an odd phrase but it does somehow capture the thing I'm after.)

I confess that at this moment Adele is having an unhealthy effect on me and perhaps in some wizard-like way she planned the effect, in concert with her special effects crew, and makes it a part of her purpose. Harried by her, you see, I simultaneously encounter a powerful alienation from Kim too, an aversion, as though both are elements of the same compound, and as though it is only with Maggie Cornelius I will find the loving ease I need. (Ease v. Tact)

This of course is sickness on my part, the sickness of weakness, for mightn't I be better off still at Bourbon-on-the-Charles, alone, or steaming down to the mouth of the great grey-green greasy Limpopo River, alone, pausing now and again for rest and reflection in the frugal shade of the fever-trees set about. I might indeed. Yet it is to Maggie that my thoughts now wander, perhaps inevitably, and I picture the two of us someplace cool, like under her bedroom window, with a cool beer on the floor beside her mattress and Maggie's cool skin racing against my palms...

"Hi Dad."

...The specific image is Maggie prowling her messy kitchen in a white tee-shirt, searching high and low for the matches to light a candle. And it is nothing she *does* as she moves about, it's simply the way she is, like a slide presentation of perfect anatomy, stressing first this muscle and then the next. The buttock flexed, the buttock sitting soft and full; the leg bending to round the back thigh, the leg extended to highlight the calf—and those uncombed auburn tresses swinging as she shifts and goes. That's visual splendor, Maggie C. in that worn white tee-shirt and nothing else, that's a clean knockout for you...

"Dad, your daughter's here!"

...and that's Sadie, hollering more or less directly into my ear, mimicking her mother. I swivel my head, pleased to find it still working after the blast, and there stands my sassy-faced befreckled child, smiling up at me. Glory be to God for dappled things! I half expected to see Maggie, as described, or Sadie in skin-tight silks and layers of garish make-up.

"Hi daughter." I kiss my favorite spot on her forehead, that high meadow of faded freckles just below the widow's peak. Still my child. "I guess you got off work?"

"Huh?"

"Weren't you out baby-sitting tonight?"

"Oh yeah. Work. I get it. Yeah, Dad, gotta make a buck, you know how it is."

"What's the going rate these days?"

"Well I charge a dollar but everyone else asks for two, and gets it."

"Two bucks an hour for baby-sitting. Lemme outa here. How much work do you get?"

"I get one dollar, I said, not two. I go whenever they call. Sometimes every day."

"'They' being these Gerbers?"

"Right."

"Why don't you put them on retainer. Charge a flat 200 a month and give them unlimited mileage."

"You lost me there, Dad."

"Never mind. It's nice to see you, sweetie. You look a lot bigger to me—have you grown?"

"Since Sunday?"

"Probably not, huh? Probably it's just thinking you're bigger because of what your mother told me."

Sadie colors suddenly and has that cornered look. I have my transition, but it will be a costly one if the little lady goes into shock.

"Relax my darling daughter. Whatever you're thinking she told me can't be what she told me. It just isn't that bad. She must not know about *that* yet."

Sadie smiles and gives a light giggle, but the color remains in her cheeks.

"What *did* she tell me? That's your line, Sades. You have to say your parts."

"Why? Cause we're having a Talk?"

"Right."

"Can I have a sip of your beer?"

"Gad, I forgot it was there. It's been in my hand so long I thought it was part of my arm. But I'm afraid it's empty."

It isn't quite empty, I was just rounding down. Sadie has been sipping from my beer ever since her infancy and I never minded, I was even amused. Why do I mind now?

"I'll get you another."

"Sit a minute first, my dear. Or *can* you sit in those jeans?"

"Don't be dumb."

"Never viewed it as an option. Now what's this about your seeing an older man?"

"God. You mean Mike?"

"What's Mike's last name?"

"Palmieri."

"Yes, Mike's the one. How old is he? What's he like?"

"He's in the 9th grade, and he's real nice. What do you want to know?"

"I'm not sure. I don't want to know anything special about Mike, really. What's it like between the two of you? What do you do for kicks?"

"You mean do we neck and smoke dope?"

"That's it, kid. Do you neck and smoke dope, or what?"

"Mostly 'or what' so far. I've only gone out with him once, you know."

"Once! That's all? And already you're into 'or what'?"

Sadie is laughing now, she has relaxed her high-chinned defensive posture. The inquisition is going her way.

"We haven't really gone out at all. We just sat together at the last school assembly."

"How come two dates this weekend, then? Are you thinking of stepping up the pace to 'or which'?"

"Dad, this is unusually dumb. It's just stuff at school. It's the Christmas play, which Marge is in so I have to go anyway and then Saturday there's the Christmas prom. I don't even know if I can stand to spend so much time with Mike. I hardly know him. But it's Christmas."

"The season of charity. And events. Fair enough."

"I can go?"

"I did not say that. How about yes to the play and no to the dance? How's that sound?"

"Why? What's wrong with the Prom?"

"Good question. I don't know, little darlin', but I do feel the same concern your mother feels. You know what I was doing at the age of twelve, when I was a kid?"

"No, I don't remember. Am I supposed to remember this one?"

"Come on! Am I really such a wind-bag?"

"I was just kidding, Dad. Can't you take a joke?"

I can't, really, though she is quoting myself to me, chapter and verse. Sensitive child, Sadie my lady, I have forced humor upon her. Probably uttered those same words—I'm just kidding, can't you take a joke—a hundred times before she finally sometimes could.

"You got me, Sades. Seriously, though, it's hard for us old fogies to see this Prom stuff starting so early. I was still into male bonding at the age of 21."

Sadie blanches. I think she believes I have just confessed to a homosexual past, but she is afraid to ask and confirm her fears. I'm not even sure what male bonding is personally, just a term

I've heard afloat on the waters of our time, the sort of suddenly-cropping-up-in-every-conversation phrase I most despise. And somehow I can't help feeling that merely to employ such a term is to ridicule it roundly, no special inflection required, though I suppose the irony may be a bit obscure for Sadie.

"When I was your age...God! I've been making up paragraphs like that for more than 10 years, haven't I? To Will and you. Do you hate it?"

"No, Dad, I'm interested, usually."

"Extraordinary."

It has crossed my mind for the first time, in this my 41st year to heaven, that I may be and indeed may always have been a colossal bore, the classical braying ass. Part of my middle-aged man crisis or part of the sorry truth? Sadie awaits the rest of the story, however, and fearful that the telephone may at any moment call her away, I put my shoulder back to the wheel of narrative.

"Twelve. I was twelve the year the Merry Mailman came to our neighborhood. Ever hear of the Merry Mailman?"

Sadie has not; she half thinks I am pulling her leg. I had forgotten him myself. Used to be on TV in the days of Buster Brown and Tom Corbett Space Cadet, Francis the Talking Mule and Captain Video with his Video Rangers. Good Lord, how very much culture we absorb, how very much evaporates. Ten thousand brain cells a day, reader, down the tubes.

"He was just a guy on TV, sort of like Mister Rogers dressed up as a mailman. But he came to give a Live performance at our neighborhood movie-house and it got turned into a huge plot. I don't know how it happened but every kid knew about it and no parent had the slightest inkling. We all showed up at the theatre with tomatoes and soft peaches ... somehow it had been decided that we ought to throw *food* at the Merry Mailman when he showed up on stage that day."

"God, how dumb."

"Yes indeed. Many times have I told you how people in groups or crowds can do things that no one of them would ever consider doing alone."

"*Many* times," Sadie grins. I was always trying to prepare her for teenage life, you see, hedging, getting her ready to at the very least *recognize* peer-group madness. Rotsa ruck. "Did *you* do it?"

"Straight to the heart of the matter, my child. I did it. We all did it. Me and Johnny Kingman didn't have any tomatoes, we couldn't get hold of anything squashy, so we brought a bag of split peas to share. We flung handfuls of peas all over the people several rows in front of us. It was just enormously stupid. And the poor Merry Mailman! No one had a thing against him. How could he understand that?"

I had drifted from my subject and for a moment could not even recall what it was while I worried belatedly over the Merry Mailman's feelings. Had he fully recovered by now, decades later? Or had the experience shattered him, had he turned to the wine? Of course he may have been brave, or at the very least he may have been prepared for it. Possible to see the Merry Mailman as a cynic to whom this sort of thing might happen all the time; takes it on the chin and cashes his check next morning.

"I think I'd rather go to the Prom, thanks just the same," says my daughter.

"Yes I suppose so. But we were just kids. That was the whole point. We acted like two-year-olds."

"That's a great point, Dad."

"It isn't coming through somehow."

It certainly isn't. Locksley the great story-teller has just taken a narrative prat-fall. And the damned thing is that this is *important*. I am hovering over an absolutely vital point and I can't even locate it, much less convey it to Sadie. All I can think of is the Merry Mailman standing up there in his suit like a shell-shocked sergeant from the Confederate Army, gone utterly blank in the face of all that flying food.

"May I interrupt?"

The return of Adele. She has taken the old puttering in the kitchen routine as far as she can take it, I guess, and I am at once relieved and annoyed by the sight of her.

"Do you remember the Merry Mailman at all—TV show that used to be on Saturday mornings, I think?"

"I can't say that I do, Reese. Is that what the two of you have been discussing all this time?"

Suddenly, *finally*, it comes to me. To Sadie I have revealed nothing more than a mouldy instance of brain-cloudy behavior, which can only have served to reinforce her conviction that the Prom's the thing. And no doubt the Prom is a fine event, with its Christmas this and its Christmas that, mistletoe and boughs of holly and chaperones up the ole wazoo. No. Whatever it is Adele fears and seeks to avert, my own dogma, mired down in the pathos and bathos of my example, concerns a loss which I am hard pressed to name or describe. I think Adele is afraid of sex, of that particular branch on the tree of innocence, for it would indeed be damaging and confusing, and yes it could even end in pregnancy-before-braces, hardly a charming sequence.

But what I fear she will lose is that time of self-discovery, those crucial difficult lonely years which merely begin at 12 and which occupy the senses very differently than do the vagaries of dating. When the kid has her wits working full blast and yet is simply not old enough to enter the world, that's when the really beautiful characters are formed. It is one of the true bounties of a bourgeois society, time for the child to polish and perfect itself, and now this hurry-up life is threatening to take it away.

Sadie is going to spend much of her time for most of her life thinking about men, bending to the thoughts or resisting them and making myriad minute judgments about "feelings" and "priorities" and "relationships", all those awful bland nouns. The truth is that once you sign on for this hitch you are on for good, one year to the next, one notion after another. You can change partners or even genders, but rarely can you change the rules of the game. As in a street fight, you cannot throw one punch (or absorb one punch) and expect to retire; you must fight to a conclusion. And the conclusion of the waltz of love comes late in life, if at all.

Why not start late too? Why not save up those years and maybe even savor them a little, when a kid bicycles to the shore, to a favorite rock or tree, and writes in her journal, alone? There will be plenty of time for the other stuff later, best to look on from a distance and wonder about it all now. The balance is wrong if you begin at 12, or even 15, there isn't a thick enough slice of that achingly delicate course *between* innocence and experience.

The matter is so clear now in my mind that I glance over half expecting Sadie to have mastered it already, by osmosis. It is such a strong, simple truth, so dense in the very air around us, that she must feel it too! Whereas in fact, of course, she has grown bored and restless, and now that her mother is here our Talk has officially concluded. She wouldn't hear me if I tried again to spell it out and in any case I cannot begin to; it is too large, too abstract.

"Can I go or not?" she asks. So, she has been putting up with me all along in the hope that good manners will beget a more generous attitude toward her Prom tickets in the end.

"Where?" says Adele.

"This weekend."

"Oh."

To me there seems no special sense in forbidding the school play and I am on the verge of a soft defeated response to the dance question. I am all set to blurt out something liberalish, partly to avoid the clash but also as a strategem. Maybe tell her she can go this once, but starting New Year's only one night per month, no later than eleven, and never with 9th graders. A trick in the guise of a compromise. You give up something specific, something right to hand and badly sought after, by way of ruling out something general in the future. Lacking the future sense, the kid accepts gratefully, even deliriously (hugs and kisses!) and signs away the right to argue the matter any further. Locksley the artful diplomat. But my heart lags so far behind the words that it drags them down at the mouth of my mouth, and what I say instead is,

"No."

And there it is, that face! This time I fear she may actually spit. Adele is bowled down onto the sofa by the sheer force of this drama, I plough ahead with loving tact.

"No, honey. We have decided against the Prom for you. I'm sorry, because I know you think you really want it badly, and that it is important to..."

"I hate you," interrupts Sadie.

"...And if I thought you would listen, I would try to explain why to you, because it is for your sake entirely..."

"I hate you both. And I'm going to go."

"No, honey. It's a no."

Sadie has flown. Out the door, into the flailing snow, no coat, no hat. Because she knows I will chase her for slamming the door, she takes no chances and simply leaves it ajar. Adele and I sit listening to the muted thump of Will's basketball on the snow and the rattle of the metal rim. Arctic wind blasts into the room and seems to fill it in mere seconds.

"Shit," is all I can think of to say or feel.

"Maybe we should let her go," says Adele.

"I don't think so. Certainly not because she got loud about it."

"No, you're right there. It's just that I have to live with her, Reese. She'll be seething at me for days, for weeks."

"Maybe. Let her think it over, though. She might surprise us."

"You expect so much from her. She's only a child."

"I want to leave," I blurt out. "I'm leaving." These words simply escape me, they are not truly spoken; I feel like the ventriloquist's dummy.

"All right, Reese. But I'm going to tell Kim. I've decided."

"Tell Kim what?" She has snapped me awake with this puzzler. What can Adele possibly wish to share with Kim concerning Sadie and her dance, or Will and his 76ers?

"About us. That we fucked."

"She knows, Dell. It was many years ago, you know."

"I mean tonight. I'll tell her that we did it again tonight."

"Why tell her that?" I say incredulously. What can be the source of Adele's many strange symptoms this evening? She keeps clawing at me and I really don't know why.

"Why not tell her that? What's the dif?"

"Truth?"

"But she'd believe me, that's what makes it true. After all, we could do it and *not* tell her. Where would the truth be then?"

"She won't believe you, Dell. I'll tell her you're a sickie."

"She'll hit you over the head with a banjo, no matter what you say. She'll believe me."

"Fuckit. Who cares. Tell her. Tell her anything you want, tell her it's April in Paris. What's it all about anyway?"

My disgust is real, not a ploy, and it has mostly to do with Sadie whom I thought we had gathered to discuss—now we have to find her. I'm not disgusted with Adele herself, but with life when it shows us so shameless. So goddamned complicated, so hard between people, even when they love.

"Sorry, Reese. I guess I carried it too far. It was meant to be a joke. Don't mind me."

Time to go, reader, you stick with me. Adele looks like Kansas awaiting the big twister. I recommend she call Berger before it hits and have him arrive shortly with a nice bottle of wine. I urge she curl up with Berger, the wine, and the late movie on CBS. I thank her for the beer and assure her we will talk again soon about the children.

I am out. The storm is wild now, clouds of snow ripped by wind. I can't see Willie in the driveway below though he is less than twenty feet away. I trace him by the sound of the ball and the creaking of the backboard struts. Down here in the horseshoe there is some shelter from the wind. I step around Will and sneak away with a rebound.

"Foul," he insists.

"No way."

"Over the top. You were on my back. Loose-ball foul. You want to play a little one-on-one, Dad?"

"No, my son, I want to hit the road while there still is one. And I want you to pack it in soon too—enough is enough."

"Not enough is not enough, too. It isn't even ten yet."

"It's close."

"There won't be any school tomorrow, either."

"Soon, though, Willie. Fifteen more minutes. Have you seen your sister?"

"She came home over an hour ago, Dad. Didn't you see her?"

"I did, but she has since escaped."

Will shrugs. I throw an arm around his shoulder and pull him to me in a hug. He whistles another foul on me for this, and grins. I still don't see Sadie anywhere and I am worried about her. She has never done anything crazy or dangerous in the past, but it is late and stormy and she is out there in nothing but a gingham shirt and jeans. I certainly will not leave without finding her. I holler twice, then I spot her; sitting in my car, in the passenger seat, staring glumly ahead.

"Hey. You wish to continue our Talk?"

No response.

"You wish to discontinue our Talk?"

No response, slight involuntary smile.

"You wish to go to the Prom with *me*?"

"Come on, Dad, it isn't funny."

"Possibly not. If you don't want to talk, how come you're here?"

"Cold out."

"There's a house. There's your room."

"I hate Mom."

"You hate us both. I heard you say so."

"I know it was her. She made you say no, didn't she?"

"Sorry, babe. I am a bit confused about this whole business, what to think or say, but that was me saying no. I really feel it's the right answer, for important reasons. Do you want to hear them?"

"I've heard them," she says, with the original world-weary sigh.

Can this be true? Can she already know in some simpler truer form all the labors of my moral soul, and is this because and only because all thought is trite? Have I finally nothing "special" to say to Sadie, on my special day?

"From whom have you heard them?"

"Never mind, Dad. I don't feel like hearing reasons at the moment."

"Sadie Marie Locksley, you are *glad* I said no!" I declare this with abrupt certainty, I am sure I have read her. "Tell the truth, you're just putting on a big act. The truth is you don't want to go to this dance at all—you just don't want to have to tell Billy Palmieri that you can't go to it, that you aren't *allowed*."

"His name is Mike Palmieri."

"That's it, though, isn't it? You never wanted to go dancing with those big kids, and having to act grown up and cool with them. Listen: tell old Mike you forgot you had to take care of Benny on Saturday night. You *could* come to the hop, only you *can't*—see the difference? Tell him you simply turn out to have More Important Things To Do. And do come take care of Benny. We'll stay home and help you take care of him. It'll be a cinch, he'll be sound asleep the whole time. The hell with the Gerber Baby, we'll give you your two bucks an hour."

"Dad..."

She looks awfully sweet, my Sadie does, arranging her mouth in that low flat impatient way.

"It's not a bribe, just a business proposition. Think about it."

She accepts a hug from me, even returns it in kind if not in degree, and she seems much improved. Have I struck upon the truth here, or have I merely provided her with an avenue for gracious escape? I have gone one-on-one with her and held my own, regardless, held her to a tie. She may just be cold, of course, or too tired to keep it up; she may have remembered something fun to do in her room. Sadie Locksley will not say, that much I know, she will very likely say nothing at all. But she has chosen not to sulk, reader, and this to me is purely a gift from the Gods. If she sulks, I leave confused and disheartened, it's as simple as that; but she doesn't. She dashes into the house to continue her life, and I leave uplifted. The world is flooded with snow and I am on my way to Maggie.

## When Donkeys Sing

As I tack down Bushmill Road toward Route 2, I ought to be sorting out my feelings about Will and Sadie. I came out this way, after all, to worry about them and yet I seem inclined to worry about their mother instead. Will's a nice lad, he's got a head on his shoulders, and he knows what he wants to do with his time. What more do you ask of a boy his age? At least you will not find him down at the Arcade emptying his brains into his fingertips like everyone else in this crazed society.

And one cannot overlook the impressive irony of these alleged predicaments, for here we had two "enlightened" parents striving from the very start to insure that their offspring grow free of all the traditional limitations of gender, always so quick to stress my aunt the doctor or Adele's sister the successful attorney. No we never bought Willie a dress but by God we might have done, if he'd asked. Yet here we have them, Will the athlete and Sadie the babysitter agonizing over a Prom date. At the very least, it leaves a person to wonder!

I ought, as I say, to be considering the kids but except for a few stray thoughts I am not. I am considering Maggie Cornelius, who is waiting for me in her Somerville duplex. Waiting and not waiting, for Maggie never wastes her time *merely* waiting. She will be there all right, but she will not have been twiddling her thumbies by the telephone. When I arrive she will not complain that it's late, she will be taken aback for I have come just a moment too soon, she is right in the middle of something. Unflattering, perhaps, yet ever so peaceful, the low-pressure rendezvous.

What I would really like is to get Maggie out here somehow, get her to meet me at Walden or Sandy Pond so we can frolic on the ice together. The immaturity theme if you will, a leitmotif of sorts. But if I call her from a phone booth and propose such a course, Maggie will not come. She would need to borrow a car, for starters, and she hates both cars and borrowing. The hour is late and the idea impractical (hmmm, she does like impracticality) but the crux of it is that basically Maggie wants to be out and about in the daylight, in or near her house by dark. That is why she won't come. She won't want to.

If I was stuck out here, of course, she'd come like a shot. I could roll the car lightly into a snow-bank, or douse the spark-plugs with a dollop of snow. I could invoke Adele's Rule and simply *say* I'm stuck, to get my way. That would be best, wouldn't it, getting my way without getting a ton of scrap metal locked into a snow-bank late at night?

It would not be best. For one thing, I wouldn't get what I want, cause what I want is fun and Maggie miffed might not be any. Oh she might laugh at my ruse and learn to like it once she was out here and saw how pretty the pond was, but I doubt it very much. And anyway, I can't invoke Adele's Rule because I voted it down scant moments ago, and I don't care for it in the least; I'm simply making merry with it as I slither over the slick roadways. I don't want to lie to Maggie, there's absolutely no need. She doesn't lie and she never seems to mind the truth. Besides which I dislike lying in general and rarely stoop to it, though it has been said of me that I omit much. Still, if Kim asks me later tonight exactly where I have been, I may very well tell her the truth. I think I will!

I would have told her about Bourbon-on-the-Charles, you know, when she asked earlier at the Hall, except that we would both have been cheapened by the process of explanation. And the whole experience would have changed in the telling. It was a small but private occasion that would have been soiled by explanations, especially since explanations generally germinate into rants at room temperature. But I didn't lie to her, I merely omitted a mention. See the difference?

That's what Benny always says, my little guy. He loves to explain things to us, explains the workings of complex machinery with wonderful simplicity. "Know how the car goes, Pa? You step on the gas!" Or enlightens us all with his delightful metaphysics: "Know what water is, Pa? Water is *water*!"

Lots of times he will explain things to us in terms of contrast and comparison, a familiar enough technique, classical technique really. He did something of the sort for Kim's father when the distinguished ambassador's car threw a rod on the Mass Turnpike last summer. "My papa's car got stuck and they towed it to the fixing place. But your car can't get fixed, so they'll tow it somewhere else instead, right Grandpa?" And once he has drawn the lines of contrast with brutal clarity, Benny always concludes with his worldly shrug for punctuation and the all-embracing refrain, "See the difference?"

Of course I would be perfectly within my rights, and my right mind, should I conclude that Kimmo does not deserve to know the truth, that she forfeited the privilege back in 1976 when she broke my 5-string banjo. She broke it over my head, reader, in an incident referred to by Adele as "the Bicentennial Fuck".

It had been hypothesized that we would take life as it came, I and Kim, remaining open to it and with each other. There would be no need for skulking around, such secrets could be shared. And so it was I alluded to the trivial business of the Bicentennial Fuck, half convinced that Kim would smile at the idea, she would locate the tiny life-loving chuckle which lay at the base of it; except my bride did not surprise me pleasantly that day. She has sometimes claimed it was being newly pregnant that made the thing intolerable to her, sacrilegious really, whereas I suspect the emotion may have been a dash more quotidian than she cared to admit. Mean green jealous is what she was, it can happen to Lyle the Crocodile it can happen to Kim. Did I actually doubt it?

So she knocked off two birds with one stone that night, liberated by violence from both the sharpest edge of her temper and the dullest of entertainments. One does not necessarily *expect* violence from the ambassador's daughter, with training in the arts of palliation, from the Laureate of Locksley Hall, so deeply steeped in the humanist sensibility. And yet, Pow! Ever had your skull crushed by a 5-string, reader? If so, you know as well as I the force and the painful shock, also the strange Bartokian discordance that flows from strings so unceremoniously unstrung, the beautiful music of dissolution and chaos that I can hum you note for note to this day.

Truth is, the review of that aftermath is causing me to reconsider now the whole question of honesty. I want to be honest but do I want to be skulled with a wok, skewered with a broom, or even have hurled at me my bride's new Smith-Corona Portable Electra 120? I do not. So I have encountered a conflict within myself and my instinctive response to all difficult issues is to draw back from them at once, and decide to decide them later. Why make hard choices before we have to? Accepting for purposes of discussion the postulate that we all must die, does it not then stand to reason that in the end, whenever it comes, we will have had fewer tortuous choices to make? Fewer, naturally, by the precise number of tortuous choices still under deferment at the official time of death.

Death does not seem imminent at the moment, however, for I have reached Route 2 and it appears passable, the one ploughed lane more or less maintained by a light steady traffic headed east into town. Of course you can't kill off your narrator anyhow—so many options swept away once one has agreed to the egregious first person voice. Too bad in a way. I mean death from exposure, in his mad dash to Maggie, in hot pursuit of "himself"? And stranded to slowly freeze in an agonizing descent into incoherence, found next morning breaking sunny and clear over the pristine landscape in the form of a literal snow-man! (He did say he wanted to go out and play in the snow, recalls ex-wife A.B. Locksley...)

Alas I must abandon this richly appropriate conclusion to my story, my life, and resume it in the middle. And now it is clear I am going to make it to Maggie's house, I realize that for the last ten minutes or more I have been hunched tensely over the wheel. I make a conscious effort to relax, measuring off long breaths and letting my mind drift pleasantly to the hour I passed at Bourbon-on-the-Charles, and for a second I almost wish I was heading back there now, instead of keeping to my unrelenting schedule. Yet one must know oneself and even today I know I could never move into a bar, never become an habitué of any such place however pleasant or in- spirational. The magic is in the moment as well as the place, I realize that, and I can count my blessings as sharply as my curses.

It is not hard to imagine the painfully mundane alternatives to my life. I am en route to the bed of a beautiful woman, later to the bed of another beautiful woman, to wake come morning to the glad and ringing madness of a small child's vast needs. But I can readily imagine that no such things exist for me, that I am one of the unlucky ones, a lonely single soul with no options. Can't find a woman I love, who loves me too, maybe can't even want to find one. Have no kids or lost them bitterly in the tilted rink of divorce-court hockey. Hate my shitty little job...

Maggie never has been married, you know. Once she was on paper, to a guy she barely knew. This was back in what Maggie has characterized almost blushingly as her "Bohemian Days" and it was one of those Vietnam ones; married men were deferred from the Army up to a point and she was willing to bail this guy out by "marrying" him. She can't remember his name, or pretends she can't. Certainly she has no idea where he is now. I suppose she's still married to him technically, but Mag's not afraid of computers like the rest of us. She contends they are like dogs, they only come after you if you act scared. She doesn't pay any taxes, either.

As for real marriage, mi casa su casa marriage, she has never seen the appeal of it. As far as I can discern, marriage has about the same emotional impact on Maggie as suburbs have on Kim: different forms of surrender and death, giving rise to the same phobic aversion. Bourgeois life seems so bleak to Maggie she feels it is Wrong to bring children into it wittingly. She doesn't agree that children are the whole point of it. She is 32 years old now and by rights she ought to be part of that syndrome of women who must fulfill their destiny soon by bearing one child before it is too late. Who do not exactly panic but do inevitably choose to make compromises of one sort or another in order to have the child in their 30's. Maggie may well feel some of that, I expect she does, yet she is nowhere close to yielding to it. According to her way of seeing, if you have the kid you will soon enough compromise everything because it is insidious, sweeps us all under one rug, the lion and the lamb, Marxists and Benthamites alike.

I and Maggie did submit ourselves to a facsimile of conventional married life for one week back in September, when she

accompanied me to the Art of the Novel Symposium at
Capistrano, Indiana. My very first symposium. My first public
appearance of any kind, as a matter of fact, for I had always in
the past declined to sign books, talk with talk-show hosts,
speak out for the Arts, or accept prizes in person. (I have
never objected to accepting them either by proxy or through
the mails, would they were forthcoming!) So why this sudden
change?

That is what Kim asked, naturally enough, and I could not
very well tell her the answer, so I omitted it. And not wishing
to substitute any false or misleading answers, for such would
constitute lying (even a shrug would do as much through the
false implication that I didn't *know* the answer) I responded
with an ancient strategem, I asked *her* a question and it turned
out to be the very question that would erase her own; to wit,
did she wish to accompany me to Capistrano, Indiana? She did
not wish to and now happily dropped the subject altogether,
perhaps satisfied that my purpose was undiscussible, as when I
am out "gathering material" for a book.

So it was that I and Maggie were thrown together. And at
once, before the journey could even commence, we faced our
first conflict, never guessing it was also destined to be our last.
It made sense to fly, of course, since we were going far away
for a short time, but Maggie draws the line at airplanes. I
knew her for a pest about motors in general—she would probably live without refrigeration if she ever got on to the fact
there's a motor somewhere inside making the coldness
possible—and yet refuse a chance to wing our way to
Capistrano? She was resolved, however, and although I
debated the point at some length with her, she did not debate
it with me.

I would like to report that we compromised happily, for example that we went by magic carpet, swift and airborne yet
quiet and safe as a means of travel. Or even that the train

schedules finally worked out, for I love a train and Mag does too, as it happens. But I must level with you—we boarded a bus. Compendium of small tortures, the bus to Indiana, penance for what? Disdain such transport, reader, disdain the very trip if you must, you will be far happier in the bathtub at home.

Which is not to say we were without amusements. For one thing I learned on the first leg of our journey, to Scranton, that the character of my fellow man was even more curious than I had suspected or portrayed it. We had been lurching along for several hours, at least five, when at last the driver mercifully announced there would be a half-hour rest-stop. Odd to "rest" when you have been sitting stock still all day, yet right on target nonetheless. We stretched our cramped legs and wolfed down huge portions of open air (God forgive the air on that bus, someone had conditioned it), then rambled off into a nearby copse of oak, full range of flaming reds and yellows. There were train tracks at the edge of the forest, rusted and grown over with ragged thistle. We felt like colts turned out of the barn in the morning, as more or less we were that week.

But there were 50 passengers on that bus to Scranton, reader, 50 colts in the barn, each one offered the same chance to frolic outside in that brittle sun and wind, and yet excepting the handful who never disembarked the bus at all, every one of the other colts entered like so many cattle to the stockpen a dreary jerrybuilt terminal to buy hot water labeled "coffee" from vending machines and then sit in rows of interconnected fiberglas chairs to drink down the unappealing liquid. And then filed back in the same orderly fashion to their seats for six more hours of bus.

I tell you what I saw, I cannot guess at what it means. A few no doubt are old or infirm and travel merely to arrive, to complete the journey. But the rest of them? We are not born solely that we may die, there are fruits to gather along the way. Those people in the plastic chairs, beyond the wavy plastic panels of the terminal wall, what can be their notion of what they wish to have from life? Should I have offered each of them a copy of my early puerile essay "Existence Precedes Rot" to arm them with silly straw-man arguments against the inevitable moments of existential defeat? Should I have charged for these copies?

For us at any rate, it was on to Indiana, where surely we did thrive. Romance and domesticity both were ours, the perfect six-day marriage. Released from a workshop on Problems of Pacing in the Epic Novel, I found Maggie darning her socks, while mine were washed and hung on a cord spanning the bathroom walls. Quite crushed by considerations of The Circe Symbol in the Novel of Quest, I was fully revived by the sight of Mag in her glasses, a first for me as she only wears them to do crosswords. Another first, Mag in the morning; hair spilled richly on the pale blue sheets and daylighted, the crusty corners of her eyes. She sleeps with her head sandwiched between two pillows, like giant earmuffs, and she brushes her teeth with baking soda. When she has a bad dream she flips on the light and reads for an hour, and most of her bad dreams are about her dog Felix getting squashed. She had a dog squashed on her once, when she was a kid, and in the dreams Felix is always both that dog and himself, and the driver never stops.

In Capistrano, or just outside it, we had found a string of cabins for rent, with small yards, perfect for us. We stumbled across the Ideal Diner for breakfast—fresh sausage, home-fries, wheat toast with strawberry preserves, and rich smoky coffee all for only $1.65—and the Green Street Market for homemade lunches, Rudy's for cheap tasty nicely lit dinners. And we agreed about everything without even trying. You may note the vivid contrast between this sweet harmony and the ceaseless strife between I and Kim in Europe, so I must hasten to say that this owes far more to circumstance than to personality. I and Kim have traveled together since, of course, and though that trauma did trail after us for a while like a portentous cartoon cloud, we have enjoyed sparkling times from Quebec to Chesapeake Bay.

Which alters not the fact that I and Maggie had it rare in Capistrano. We got along too well, if anything, it was almost eerie how everything struck us in the exact same way. Not just the relentless pretensions of the literati in symposia—for if "donkeys set to work at singing, you're sure enough what the tune will be"—but every shrub and painted sign, every blast of foundry air, even the grim beauty of the red-eye special from Toledo to Scranton or the sad necessity of a microwave egg. Yes even the very dregs of travel, the stale and weary way *back*, proved nothing but fun for I and M.

Of course it was a limited proposition, we were coming back and we knew it, M. to her world, and I to mine. Still to me it seemed largely a matter of theory and practice. In theory, Maggie could not abide marriage, in practice she'd be very good at it. You'll judge for yourself soon enough as I am by now back in the city, skirting the Arlington line, cruising through Powderhouse Square, and gearing up for a run at Maggie's hill. Between the red lights and the slow skids, however, I think we may have just enough time for this little story about Maggie, though it's more a story *about* a story about Maggie, as you'll see.

This nagging business of stories within stories may wear on you at times, you may feel you are being subjected to a veritable shmoo of a book, but the simple fact is the more I tell you the more you'll know. The benefit we hoped to have from this albatrocious first-person, remember, was that at the very least you would know and understand me. My heart would be on my sleeve, my feelings on the line and not in be-tween the lines. There will be no "Reader's Guide" to the

volume at hand, perhaps for other reasons as well; but there is
no need, the work explains itself, laboriously.

So just a word, if you will, about the story about the story
about Maggie. This is actually a story I wanted to write and
tried to write, but it "wasn't". This happens sometimes, according to Winnie-the-Pooh, because stories "aren't things
which you get, they're things which get *you*" and all you can
do is go where they can find you. I tried that too and as yet
the story has not managed to ferret me out. But in it, happen
it were writ, a young man in an office meets a striking new
employee, a pretty, lively woman who is forthcoming with
him from the first. There is no doubt she flirts with him,
seems to encourage him, though she is admittedly flirtatious
in general, as part of her liveliness. He is bashful, however,
and so rather than speak up and take his chances with her, he
internalizes the matter and begins to examine every speech and
motion minutely, laboring every nuance throughout the
workday so that it is a constant issue with him, an obsession.

Of course he assumes the same is true for her, and that one
of them must take the leap soon, and declare. He comes close
each day and as the tension builds we are by turns rooting for
him, annoyed with him, fearful for him. Until at last he learns
he has misconstrued the situation altogether, that she has been
for weeks involved with someone else in the office. She is
simply friendly, outgoing, and moreover glowing at him with
her ardor for the other man. And though all this is common
knowledge, it has never even grazed his mind as a possibility.
For him there were only two actors in the play and two potential denouements: she shared his desire, or she didn't quite.

In the hands of Thomas Mann we would have had from this
sad little dance a grand cadenza, from Dostoevsky no doubt a
blood crime, from Hawthorne or Maupassant a small pithy
moralism. From Locksley we got a small pissy muddle, or
mud-puddle, because it simply wasn't, as previously stated.

But that's another story. This one's about Maggie C. and me,
and it goes like this right here, a one-two-three-four   a-one-

I met her last summer at Benny's day-care. She knew several
of the parents there and had been asked to do some drawing
with the kids. They were transfixed when I came in that afternoon, I never saw such calmness and productivity, least of all
toward the end of the day. Instead of climbing the walls, they
were all sitting at tables cranking out surprisingly faithful like-
nesses of God's creatures — dogs that looked like dogs, horses
that looked like horses! — and feeling by the way immensely
pleased with themselves. Perched up on one of the deep
window-sills, Maggie commanded the scene quite casually in
fact, but she struck me at once as a sudden thunderbolt of
grace and beauty, sending a genuine electric jolt to my senses,
though she remained herself the very prototype of composure,
silently bespeaking her obvious and absolute knowledge of exactly who she was and wished to be.

I could not fail to speak. Had I let her escape at that moment, and never glimpsed her again, I would have felt like a
poor man and that bewitching vision of her an unforgettable
gilt-edged memento of my poverty. True I asked her for the
proverbial cup of coffee but be not too hard on me, it was
enough I found my feeble tongue. And the wonder of it was
the bargain was already struck, we both were sold on first
sight. I was, as indicated, but she was too. Impossible luck!

How could such a woman be available, much less on the
difficult basis I needed her to be available — no strings at-
tached, stolen moments in smoky places, don't call us we'll
call you sort of availability? She didn't care a fig. We would
see each other when it was possible, she would be happy and
busy when it was not. And she was without question the
busiest human being I have ever known, by the way, rather a
remarkable feat for someone with no family to care for and no
steady job either.

So there we were, and we proceeded. Our emotions seemed exactly in balance, our affection and need for each other expanded with our comfort as a couple. The physical surprises were all pleasant and yet the sense I had at the start, that such luck did not exist in the world as I knew it, that sense never left me. Partly because of how Maggie is, I always had the feeling she might burst at any moment, or evaporate and escape like steam. As the weeks went by, however, she did neither, burst nor evaporate. She remained the same, warm-blooded lover, soft-hearted friend.

How was this possible, I wondered incredulously, all the while wallowing in the acute luxury the rich must feel while they are getting richer. How could she simply be mine? Well, of course, she was and she also wasn't, for like my young man in the story about the story, I had failed to take everything into account. Maggie, not so surprisingly, had another fella too. See the difference?

## Beast in the Jungle

Maggie's street cuts across the highest hill in the town of Somerville, from the top of which one can behold twenty square miles of almost systematic ugliness. At the top, however, there is a lovely old castle, an unexplained granite edifice with barred windows, two jutting turrets, and winding stone stairways, that stands empty but accessible to children playing hide-and-seek, young lovers who would scribble their initials, and all those sundry individuals who in passing such a place will automatically ascend, gaze, and dream a moment before continuing along.

The houses on her block, which is called Rockland Terrace, are so close together that abutters might well faire amour without ever leaving their respective domiciles; possible to arrange and commit infidelities while one's spouse lounges in the tub all unknowing! The music and entertainments of one home are visited willy-nilly on the four others that have it surrounded. Yards comprise half a dozen to a dozen carefully set flagstones and a brace of plastic cherubim fringed with pitiful flowers, the lot resolutely bordered by chain-link aluminum. All this, mind you, scant seconds away from McDonald's fast hamburger, Papa Gino's fast pizza, and Arthur Treacher's fast fish!

Tonight the dogs are barking on Rockland Terrace. They run at my heels, four or five of them, and flare their gums to show the teeth. This is not usual. I have never seen so many dogs on the block before, and it pops in my mind that there must be a full moon. Though I mean nothing by this, I am startled to discover that above the twin round turrets of the castle the vaulting moon is indeed bright and full. The entire sky has been thoroughly transformed, or magically replaced by a different sky, no longer white and wild but molten black like a huge bowl of oil.

Inside the gate I am surprised as always by the sight of Maggie's bike—the ongoing miracle goes on. You see, Maggie refuses to bind the bike cruelly with chains and cables, says she'd only lose the key. Yet this is a rare and wonderful machine, a German touring bike built to last in 1930 and with all its sturdy, substantial (if slightly military) appointments still in perfect fettle. What is loose is gone nowadays, but Mag likes to lean it against fences or porch-railings and trust to the best in human nature, or perhaps to the element of surprise.

I know there is a theory that thieves assume nothing of value will be unprotected and are therefore attracted to difficulty. And no doubt there was a grain of truth in tales of the garbageworkers' strike in New York City years ago. (To dispose of trash during the strike people reportedly wrapped it up neatly and locked it in the back seat of a car; in the morning, gone.) Still by rights that bike should be stolen. I mean, the damned thing is just sitting there. I could climb on it right now and be a mile away in minutes without even pedaling. If I pedaled, I could make it to the Mexican border by sunrise. I know if it were *my* bike it would vanish instantly, as I don't have her sort of luck, faith of the fairies confirmed by the Gods sort of luck.

Mag's desk is downstairs on the street side, in a bay window that juts out alongside the front porch so the bay is almost like a jeweler's show-case and through the nearest window of the three, the one angling away from her front door, one can often watch Maggie at her paperwork. This arrangement has at times seemed mildly lunatic to me, because the city is a jungle freely roamed by beasts of prey, yet I agree with Maggie that it is also crazy to let your life be shaped by fear of other people who are in *fact* crazy.

She doesn't lock doors either—as I'll wager you've guessed already, for she is as consistent as she is impractical—so I could simply walk in with a view-halloo instead of waiting. I prefer to rap on the windowpane, however, and I don't always rap right away. I am fascinated by her obliviousness. There she sits, bright-lit and clear, and I see her in such sharp focus that I cannot help assuming she sees me too, or at least senses my presence. What with the streetlight and the porch lamps above me I may even cast a shadow through the glass into her room, but Maggie never sees me or hears me over her music till I have rapped insistently for a time.

So I do, and her own dog howls, and a throaty neighbor cries out for quiet, and Maggie continues, head down, poised and exceptionally lovely, absorbed in her letter-writing, and I must keep on till quite suddenly it permeates her concentration and I see her leap up and literally run to the door. It's all a secret to her, she thinks she is responding promptly!

The door flies open, Felix comes crashing into my midsection, and I and Maggie are holding each other. And for a time nothing will be said, while Felix pushes at us with his snout and tries to worm his way between, like a child. It is luxurious simply being close, like climbing into a tub of steamy water when you're trail-dusty, or a fresh-made bed when you're spent. For a moment Mag may seem smaller than I recalled, her face more delicate or her hands less smooth. Perception plays its tricks, though only for a moment.

"You went after all," she says.

"Sure."

"I was afraid you might not go, with the storm. So that you might not come, and you couldn't call..."

"You cared?"

"What do you think, fool?" She pokes me in the belly for emphasis. "Was it awful?"

"It was magnificent," I reply, knowing full well that only a groan-up in a car-car could conceive the notion a "bad" storm.

"It was hailing up on the roof here. I opened the clear-story and it came in like moth-balls."

"There's an incredible moon. You want to walk out and see it?"

"In a bit. Let's go up for a hug first."

I cart her upstairs piggy-back, her head resting on my shoulder, her mouth softly kissing my neck. In her bedroom I lower us down onto the mattress so that I am lying on my belly on the bed, she is lying on her belly on my back. She scrabbles across me to the bedside table and lights the fat dripping candles. Then we roll apart most business-like and start to toss the clothes aside. The clothes are not useful in this situation and to retain them, even a single raiment for a solitary moment, would be error. The scratchy, binding and confining cloth is simply no match for the smooth cool perfect-fitting skin.

I and Maggie will again have nothing to say, for the next half-hour or so. If comparisons be invidious, then surely none moreso than the comparison of lovers, one to another. But to compare situations is different and I have noticed that I and Kim are very apt to talk while we make love, to joke mostly, to make a suggestion, declare a preference, or announce a momentary discomfort. Sometimes merely to sigh or exclaim. With Mag there will be no sound at all, save the final gasps. It is not entirely that speech would be superfluous, or that it would be dwarfed by the grandeur of our passion, washing over the scene like a Sibelius symphony. I am often in the dark, candle-power notwithstanding, as to Maggie's exact status or inclination at a given moment and though I know I will not inquire, I do not know whether this is because the love-making is to her too holy or altogether too unholy for such matters to be broached.

So saying nothing we set about it, below the soft nest of near translucent snow that has drifted against the window sash, in the streaming moonlight no less, groping somewhat hungrily (for there has been an interval) and arranging and re-arranging our bodies to insure every subtlety of earthly delight. However we thrash and swirl in the inevitable hope-less tangle of sheets and blankets, the pillows stripped of their cases, the corners of the striped ticking bared, still we end up quite typically with Mag in the saddle, riding to glory. I move my palms lightly over her nipples and down the smooth flanks to help enhance her pleasure as it progresses, keenly aware that my own pleasure is effortlessly assured, and that *is* sexist, Sadie, but don't blame me, blame God. Her fingers clamp my shoulders and she sways in her trance above me, for by now we have begun to shiver Maggie's timbers properly; indeed I can feel it change and unfold those sweet final seconds as she bucks against me and takes me along to glory with her.

Another magic has been worked and still is humming softly as we collapse in a heap, the two-backed beast at leisure. Mag likes to stay there, conjoined, and it is not for me to quibble in the lap of such peace and plenty. Even now we will not say much, it will be felt as a private moment. In a way there is simply nothing to say. Certainly much that one might utter would be false, or unnecessary, or would constitute mere ner-vous chatter. Verbal endearments are out, on that we agree, and it is too soon to introduce Topics, so we lie there, close and content and bathed in such silence as the city provides.

To say that we lie "bathed in silence" would be wrong not only as trite description but also because there is no silence in the city; one sound succeeds another, as when the droning of the refrigerator relents and at once the rumble of trucks on Milk Street emerges. Sometimes, if the pigeons happen to be lighting on the sills, we can listen to the sash-weights clank against one another in the hollow of the wall. And almost any time we can hear Greta shouting to herself on the other side of the building, beyond the central chimneys.

Greta's real name is Mrs. John Charboneau, but we call her Greta because we believe she deserves a better first name than "Mrs. John", a genuine first name sort of first name. And then too she so often says that she wishes only to be left *alone*, hence Greta. As in Greta Garbo, gret it? Mister John Charboneau apparently escaped long ago, whether to death or Texas we know not, and if there were issue from the union, such issue do not deign to visit. She is a sad pathetic soul, really, and yet she resists all efforts at pleasantness so sourly that by now even to offer is a disagreeable experience. There is a certain kind of pensioned urban lady, not exactly old, who lives in dark rooms with 30 or 40 cats; Greta seems like one of those to me, only without the cats.

She keeps busy talking to herself, though, and as I mentioned the talking generally ends in shouting. She gets worked up about things, I guess. I used to assume she was shouting at us, in an attempt to constrict our love-making, but Mag learned the truth one day last August when miraculously, for the first and only time, Greta's window was open. The two bedroom windows are barely a yard apart and Maggie could hear more clearly than ever before the muttering, the mounting of sly threats, and finally the stream of foul oaths climaxing in a "No no no no no no N-o-o-ooo" sequence that sent her flying to the rescue, smashing through two of Greta's panel doors only to find herself facing not an endangered grateful Greta but rather a furious gaping Greta, appalled at the temerity of Mag's intrusion. There was no assailant in evidence. Greta was completely alone (therefore in the state she had so often expressed herself as preferring) and under no apparent threat from without despite all the hubbub. This sort of behavior helps explain Greta's craving for solitude; she would only be happy if Maggie's half of the house were let to a corpse.

"I asked Greta to tea yesterday," Maggie tells me now.

"Tea? As in high tea, four o'clock in the afternoon, lords and ladies?"

"Oh yes, all very formal," Maggie smiles.

"You printed up invitations—Miss Maggie Cornelius requests the presence of Mrs. John Charboneau at four o'clock and all?"

"Well, you see, I had a pot of tea brewing in the kitchen..."

"Excellent place to have it brewing."

"I thought she would come."

"Why ever?"

"Well it's very rare what happened, Maurice. She has that little peephole, you know, and she *never* comes out on the porch if she sees anyone there. Even if Felix is napping there, she'll wait hours just to step outside for her mail. So I thought it was meaningful, sort of an overture, when she did come out."

"And did she come to tea?"

"Oh God no. She was awful about it, all but had me arrested on the spot for dreaming up such a wild idea."

"What would you have done if she had accepted?"

"I wanted her to accept. I always think that one day, for no special reason, she will suddenly turn human. And start chatting about the weather, or reach down and pat Felix carelessly on the head..."

"Don't hold your breath."

She makes no reply but a moment later I turn to her and see that her cheeks are inflated like wind-socks. This is Maggie's joke, she is "holding her breath". You see, I am always telling her how perverse she can be, doing things for no better reason than that someone has told her *not* to do them. So she is holding her breath because I told her "not to". That's that one.

"I get it."

"*Took* you long enough," she explodes. Now she nestles against me spoon-fashion and arranges my arms around her. "Do you want to walk in the moonlight still?"

"Let's have a hug first. Tell me what you've been up to."

"First you tell me why you're so restless tonight. It's obvious, you know—something's bothering you."

"Not really. Just a trifling mid-life crisis."

"You should never trifle with mid-wifes. But tell me, is everyone okay at home?"

"Oh sure, everyone's fine. It isn't anything, it really isn't. It isn't even real, really. It isn't, even."

"Well *that's* good," she jostles me. "And I'm sure it helped to talk about it."

We must both smile at this, though I would talk about it freely if it had a talking-about aspect to it. I do not usually sit on my complaints or worries too long and if I know a great deal more about Maggie than she knows about me, it is only because she never asks questions and I never presume to hold forth on the subject of myself. (Any other subject I will happily exhaust.) But she never asks about my past, the mystery of my history. She couldn't tell you my age, though I know her very date of birth; doesn't know scoot about my parents, though I could catalogue the habits and disasters of hers; I suspect she doesn't even know where I was born and raised, and yet I could regale you for hours on her first ten years alone. She doesn't ask.

Does she not ask because she does Not Care? Does she fear Getting Hurt by too intimate a familiarity, what with Kim and all? Or is she in some utterly surprising way merely self-centered, a closet egoist? Surely the imbalance, in the area of information, has been striking. I have always probed her with artless interest, simply because she fascinates and charms me so, by her eccentricities and by the broader eccentricity of her very existence, alone in this house on Rockland Terrace.

She does disdain symmetry, like the symmetry of corresponding inquiries—what do you do/what do *you* do sort of inquiries. I am sure you could say the phrase "I love you" a hundred times to her, at all her softest moments, and she would neither say it back a single time nor feel the lack of symmetry inherent in her not saying it. She will be tender at such times, mind you, as she will be sweetly solicitous of all my ailments and concerns. It is in the past and the future that she evinces no interest.

"Stop frowning," I say, smoothing her forehead.

"Maybe you need to get away, Maurice. Go sit on the beach somewhere and brood."

"You want to take a trip with me?"

"Me? I don't even want to take a *walk* with you."

It's true, she doesn't. Mag is very basic tonight. Left to her direction, our scene for tonight might well have had no speeches at all, from arrival through departure a wordless tryst, and yet been tender at every moment. She *mistrusts* words, I think, and prefers not to rely upon them overmuch. Just so, she turns again now, pushes her bottom gently against me, and presses my hands to her breasts. She has times when she wants to get closer than close, physically, when nothing short of the transposition of skins will satisfy her desire for union.

So we have here the very portrait of tranquility, the naked figures of the lovers gently twining, yellow moon framed in the window, glowing through the wafer-thin edges of the soft piled snow, and it is perhaps striking to you (certainly it is striking to you if you have read carefully) that this romantic canvas can stand up to some of the harsh realities cited earlier. I do not refer to my family or to family life here, for you know how Maggie feels, or purports to feel, about my situation. You do not know how I feel about my situation (How could you, when I don't?) or how I feel about Maggie's. I refer to Wolfgang.

That was what I called him — funloving Locksley! — it seemed to ease the burden of having to contemplate him at all somehow. Maggie persisted in calling him "Perry" because of her aforementioned custom regarding names. But let me say a word or two around-about the subject of jealousy, as I have found the business of the Other Man especially interesting. He was indeed a matter of some consternation to me, for even the largest spirits will prefer an exclusive love when they can have it, whether or no they are providing the same in exchange. And if larger spirits prefer it, reader, what then of the likes of me, mean-spirited remorseless Locksley?

Though my love for Kim seemed undiminished by the advent of Maggie Cornelius, it was hard to believe that the converse was equally true, that Maggie's affection for me could be full and sincere when she stood by another romance as well. How could I doubt her? I could not, when we were together, but we were together very seldom. Such doubt is insidious and also self-intensifying, and can make horrible sport with a weak creature like man. I wanted Maggie to conclude her affair with this Wolfgang person, albeit he had staked a prior claim and although I neither offered nor contemplated any roughly reciprocal action. I wanted it not in any "fair" sense, but rather in the sense that it was what I wanted. And reader, I was informed that I could not have what I wanted.

Initially this seemed a disaster to me, a clear rejection. I felt like a cast-off suitor. I was certain that she had chosen against me and furthermore had left me powerless in the matter. But here an odd thing happened, for I found there is a way in which power is sometimes transferred to the powerless in affairs of the heart. You may have experienced an instance of this, where someone else is "in charge" of your relationship, and after the usual conflicts and ambiguities moves to end it. You are twisting in the wind for months and even years and then, when the break is finally made you feel some of the power return to yourself. You were subject and suddenly you are free, because the victim is always set free, by fatalism. Nothing is ever lost until a choice is made; that is what makes choice so difficult and it is why to some extent the chooser is always the loser.

This was not quite that, for Maggie had rejected not me but a presumptuous suggestion of mine, which had arisen from the pernicious reflex of jealousy. Yet by asking straight out and in being just as directly refused, I was somehow purged of all poisonous emotion. Mirabile dictu! The matter was so plainly out of my hands that it ceased to concern me at all. This may sound like sophistry but it felt genuine and utterly convincing, and as a result I was able to behave like myself again instead of some strange little knee-jerk fiend living within my body. And we were able to continue merrily along, never speaking of Wolfgang or on my part even thinking of him, until the day Maggie casually mentioned she would not be seeing him any more. That decision was a private one, it had nothing to do with me, and we never discussed it one minute. She simply passed along the upshot, and there it stands.

Now I will understand if you feel disinclined to rejoice with me over the departure of Wolfgang, for aside from the question of comeuppance there is the matter of plot. You may still have been hoping for a plot of some kind to take hold in this book and it's things like Wolfgang that give you your soap-opera potential. I do know how to write plot, you know — was there not, if anything, too *much* plot to *Éclairs for Rumpole*? With Wolfgang we had a better shot at hair-rendings and heart-breakings, all the suspense and low-lying violence of romantic rivalry. But if we consider the structure of our story, in which the protagonist makes successive visits to three women who are ipso facto in emotional conflict, with each other if not with him, something grisly might have been perfectly manageable in any case. Somewhere along the line he might kill one of these women, or one of them might kill him. (No, it's written first person, he stays.) He kills one of them, but which one? That's the thing to learn!

Trouble is, of course, it just wouldn't wash, none of it. The bland bony truth is that there can be no knife upraised and gleaming above the long white neck. We can have no Raskolnikov here, no Smerdyakov. To believe it even a tiny bit you would have to misread the character completely, or take the frivolous surface of the story to mean the underlying intent has been frivolous too.

There is a tale by Henry James, Frank and Jesse's younger brother, whom you may recall for his having recorded with ceaseless nuance the silly manners of an imagined transatlantic gentry in a series of polished high-toned soap-operas of his own — a tale called "The Beast in the Jungle", I believe, that concerns a man who spends his entire life waiting. For something to happen. To him. (As in *to* him, not as in to *him*. See the difference?) And the irony is of course that it simply is not going to happen. Whatever it is he both fears and awaits, dreads and in negation almost welcomes, it is his precise fate that nothing will ever happen to him. There is no beast on the branch above him, ready to spring and claw.

Well, nothing is something that never happens to anyone, really. Each second events occur and even the most quotidian lives have their stops and turns. And the things that do not happen are as much experiences as the things that do, for there is work and there is out-of-work, there is school and there is the lack of schooling. There are all sorts of successes and failures, among them success with the opposite sex and its opposite. We can't all be the Range Rider, or even Rudyard Kipling, tant pis, yet it remains the case that the fellow in this story, our eye, is the Beast in the Jungle sort of fellow, roughly, and though much has happened to him in his life, there is also a plane of perception on which nothing has, and certainly nothing akin to the brutal removal of Maggie C. or her ilk from the roster of the quick. Nothing like the gleaming knife, or the dull gray gun. Sorry about that.

Instead, this character is characteristically extended across the long Cornelius legs to kiss the stray Cornelius calf and brush the lovely muscle there, then drift north (map-style) toward the quivering Cornelius core, up the strong back thigh to the startling crescent below each buttock; to part the perfect weight of those buttocks slowly, hearken to the small wet sound, and graze the twilit field between. So that soon enough the lovers have begun to move together, their hands again ranging helplessly about, and their lips, for passion is a form of helplessness, a loss of consciousness, and as an "art"— which it is sometimes termed if not downright ballyhooed— very helpless indeed, as it is ordained at its best to be artless, formless, a hunger. The two-backed beast in the jungle!

Much attention of late has come to the question of the female orgasm and to the kudos due your patient well-schooled male contestant, not merely sensitive but also richly informed by a society of technicians. This is well and good, and no less true than ever, but let us also lift a glass to unbridled passion while it lasts. There is something in a woman of real blood that seeks to be treated differently, that craves precisely passion instead of art, wants to see the mad whirling need of her even more keenly at times than she wants her own gratification in the most literal sense, and glories absolutely in deserving it, in holding the kind of power than can provoke it. So it is with Maggie, she likes to see that passion coming at her.

And so here we are on our second heat, and this time the edge is really on. In a way the first is merely an awkward hello, the second contains the bombast. It's a slow-rising agonizing tingle that has got Maggie's skin tight and lively, goose-bumps from her neck to her hips and the nipples straining brightly upward as we rock along, tracking the laser of pleasure together, till suddenly Maggie leaps ahead and now she's racing headlong at me, *she's* the one who's all unbridled, and I am simply holding on as we hurtle toward the close. And here we go...

...over. The instant is gone, which so uniquely mixes absolute power with utter helplessness, but which remains only an instant. A whipstitch. So abruptly we exchange the heart's most furious energy for the soul's most complete repose! And for some reason upstart snippets of bad home-made poetry rustle in the brush of my returning faculties—a sleek horse striving belittles the reins, the gay obliteration of the brain...Maggie's hips are silk again and now as our faces rest together I can literally feel her cheek cool, her breath and heartbeat quiet.

Together we compose a brief stanza of silence, a mere couplet this time, before launching a favorite game, where we search for animals in the patchy configurations of Maggie's plaster ceiling. Mag insists on the Bengal tiger to the right of the light fixture though I can never see it; we concur on both the rabbit and the pygmy goat and we are always expecting to find others up there. But it is brisk below the window of the rattling weights, and it doesn't take long before the post-coital cool-out becomes downright shivery. Mag grabs her tee-shirt and yanks it over her head, the very moment I have anticipated.

"Get me a beer?" I propose.

"Get it yourself. And get my toast while you're up."

You see, some people have post-coital *triste*, but not Maggie, she has post-coital toaste, always likes at least three or four slices with jam.

"Well I would if I wanted the beer. What I really want is to watch you going to get the beer. See the difference?"

She rolls her eyes at this last phrase, for she has heard it once or twice previously, as you have, but she does get up to fetch the beer and toast. I'm sure she thinks I'm kidding about watching as she springs from the bed and traverses the room in a gallant mockery of the voyeur's delight, near-nude descending the stair-case and now the return trip more shyly, toasted fig-leaf coy. But Maggie glimpsed!

You may feel that I have exaggerated, perhaps for literary effect, the Cornelius appeal. You may remind that surely "beauty" is still at best in the eye of the beholder, and never a universal proof. A few may even cavil that it is only "skin deep" and therefore hardly a matter for concern east of Beverly Hills. But really, reader, only skin deep? In the presence of Maggie C.—the gentle swell of belly, the lean shapely leg lightly fuzzed, the face that launched a thousand nights of male despair—in the presence then of such auburn and ebony detail as I have omitted to describe for fear of mere prurience, what can be the meaning of the word "only" in the phrase "only skin deep"?

# THE ROONEY PLAN

S o Wolfgang is gone before he really arrived, and in his leaving is revealed another truth I overlooked that day at the day-care. The burden was not that Maggie couldn't be mine because she might not want to, or because Wolfgang or a whole gang of Wolfgangs might stand in the way, but that Maggie simply *wasn't* mine, she was hers and moreover I was mine, or Kim's; that all this would become difficult emotionally. I was casting myself, the protagonist of record, as antagonist too and in the matter of Locksley versus Locksley one of us must lose. Too late I recalled that although the rich get richer, they also grow sour and unhappy. It was never would she have me but rather, what would become of me if she did!

Love is strange, gentle reader, Mickey and Sylvia said it best. If you chanced to spend tomorrow afternoon in the company of Maggie Cornelius, you might come away entranced but you might as easily come away indifferent, or appalled. Her attainments I have yet to touch upon and very likely they are wholly irrelevant; we may admire people for their attainments, or respect them, but unless we are groupies we do not love them for the attainments. Point is, none can know why love occurs or even what it may consist of, save to say that as an emotion it always feels sufficiently precise to the individual who suffers from it.

Well I have suffered for Maggie. That's why I'm here tonight really, because by now if I could do without her I would. But it's a visceral matter, the simple wishing-to-be-with and unhappy-at-being-without, and it can wall off your mind from the light of this world. When it has you that way, moreover, it can expand a love affair to dimensions which threaten a marriage. Does one "run off" with Maggie C. to start a "new life", or not? Swayed by the agony of her absence or loss, riddled with incorrigible illusions of well-being and pleasure, poor old Michael Finnegan begin again?

Wary, to be sure, of such change. One strives for perspective against the heart's eternal return, for there are cycles to consider, what goes around comes around, and isn't this new life just a new mounting of the old life? Aye, in my beginning is my end, and all *that*. In addition to which I am awary that Mag's appeal has at least something to do with the circumstance of her unconstraint, her childlessness. There are ways in which the rearing of children must inevitably trivialize a woman (yes Sadie, a man too), bourgeoisify her as Mag might have it, and there comes a narrowing-down of personality in the repetitive language and tasks of parenthood. The constant onslaught of duty results in a loss of vital energy which is at times an obstacle, at other times a treasured point of union and mutual understanding. But did you know that the current world record for consecutive sentences completed, uninterrupted and fully intelligible, by a groan-up to a groan-up in the American bourgeois home, is two?

So yes, Maggie C. is sleek and worldly, conveys that glossy illusion that life at each moment throbs with promise, and why not? She has only to sustain it a few short hours each week, while others are left to sort through the detritus of errands and obligations. As it happens, though, I have seen her sustain it longer, when we experienced "real life" together in Capistrano last autumn. Not the kind of real life where the vicissitudes of years wash over you and the second mortgage picks your pocket, but the kind where you are subjected to each other around the clock and must undergo all the forms of the 24-hour-day, and we proved alarmingly compatible.

I think of that sojourn in Capistrano often—it was a golden time for me, mule-hauled up out of the mud-rut I was, ate my cake and had it too on your Limpopo leitmotif scorecard—and I am thinking of it right now as a matter of fact, as we finally begin our trek over the luminous midnight snow. Riddled again with those incorrigible illusions of well-being and pleasure, beguiling promises of a sustained magic, the kind that just won't quit, I and Maggie sort of magic...

No ploughs will try the hill before morning, the Lord's will manifest in snow for six more hours. With the curbs blotted out by the contours of His storm, an actual landscape seems to live and breathe beneath the hard gray mask of civilization. We crunch our boots carelessly up the hill, side by side by side (for Felix the dog makes threee) and playfully thrash out the details of Maggie's end-of-the-world plan. Since it has to end soon anyhow, she argues, why not have the engineers devise some means of Universal Surface Explosion (call this U.S.E.) such that all at once everything is inverted, our world of plastic, cement and metal buried and the most opulent top-soil settled above it, ripe for germination. Useful or what? And the promo campaign, with the winner of the Miss USE pageant up there on the Misuse float in her bathing-suit and diagonal between-the-breasts banner!

As always when we walk, we encounter unexpected lit-up scenes. It is part of the charisma of a fresh couple that the world very kindly organizes a bit of a parade around you, life's little dramas come more sharply to your notice. So although we are in Somerville at midnight after a storm, we see four black teenaged girls striding toward us, spanning the available roadway with their arms linked together and blaring out a spirited gospel shout in rich impromptu harmonies.

> The Lord has promised
> And His word is so true.
> Just keep on praying,
> He'll answer you.

They are a sight, reader, this squadron of midnight messengers, they would be a sight anywhere with such surreal sororial harmony and gladness, but in the town of Somerville, Mass., one does not see the Negro, it's a hard-hat town. The Negro does not live in Somerville much, nor visit, and must rarely sing in the streets here late into the night. It's more magic, you see, it's all for us. God v. Devil, Tonight Only, One Show at Midnight, Get Your Tickets Early!

Maggie is fond of teenagers, says she finds something sweet and endearing in all but the worst of them. Notwithstanding my own offspring, I can only hope to learn what it is. In the past I had always assumed the point of teenagers was to scare off the flying-saucer people, to discourage them from taking over our planet. I know it will put me in trouble with Maggs but I proceed now to relate an anecdote to her, an incident I happened to witness two months back on Beacon Hill, or at the foot of it, on Charles Street.

There were three of them on this particular occasion (and that's at least half the problem, they will travel in packs), roller-skating down Charles Street on a Saturday afternoon as is the fashion for this year. Charles Street on Saturday is a circus, if you don't know it, everyone is dressing it up and trotting it out and generally celebrating whatever they liked best in this morning's mirror, and so here come these three very young men in their high black Chicago-style skates, dipping and dancing and gliding down the center of the congested boulevard to the absolutely booming and ceaselessly crashing refrain of some disco hit on the suitcase-size tape-deck which the middle skater is shouldering.

It's a cut and dried case of Assault with Batteries, but there is no denying they too are a sight, heads are turning right and left. No denying they are the spiritual millionaires of the moment, until with a cruel abruptness it is ended. Crash crash tinkle tinkle. The tape-deck has gone down and shattered, and in an almost poignant but also acutely comic tableau of silence, the three eight-footers are reduced to three little lost boys, kneeling in the street over their fallen idol and totally at a loss for any sense of future or for even the smallest shard of speech or gesture. They are as shattered and silenced as their machine.

Frozen moments, reader, blokes and their tableaux, vignettes and vinaigrettes. And I muse, though not aloud to Maggie, that it must fall upon God to punish crimes so new they are not yet on the books, that of course fate must take a hand. But speaking of hands, I was holding one of Maggie's when I launched my little anecdote and now I find I am not holding it anymore as the anecdote drops anchor. She has in the course of the anecdote, then, repossessed the hand.

"The poor slobs," she says.

"Well yes, but this was good. It was pretty rich. Hell, it was perfect."

"It's no big deal, I just can't see feeling glad it happened to them."

Is it no big deal? Am I wrong to be glad? Gee, I suppose maybe so. Poor kids, such a waste, and for what? A smile, an irony? I must be wrong to be glad, yet still I cannot lie.

"Not glad it happened to them exactly, glad it happened to *me*. See the difference? And at the time, Charles Street on a Saturday and all, who could blame me? They were just part of the show, that was their choice. Admit that one does like to see the absurd come to a reckoning."

"Maurice," she pokes me, "it simply isn't sound to relish the misfortunes of other people."

"These weren't people, these were teenagers."

"Unsound. Consider your mortal soul."

"Nothing mortal about it. Can I have back your hand?"

She hands it over, smiling at herself for she does not like being such an out-and-out moralist; she didn't realize the hand had been used to punish me, and now she does.

"Sorry."

But she is not sorry, she is appalled. She doesn't understand my sense of humor quite, or else she simply doesn't care for it. Of course she can't help being a critical person in her way any more than I can in mine, but the one disturbing strain in Maggie's personality is this, that I sometimes feel her depth of devotion and trust it, at other times I feel she would ditch me where I stand for a Wrong Opinion. She's that definite. And so, naturally enough, I cannot resist pushing all my worst opinions across the table at her, for closest scrutiny.

This one slides past and our hands are locked again, the mittens snugly mated, though I know I am sorry she didn't enjoy the scenario for its own sake and I know she is sorry I couldn't have told it with a different moral. But we are clumping over the crusty snow, and Felix is whirling in circles, pushing his front paws against our bellies in an effort to incite The Game, and of course playing The Game with Felix is the way back to Maggie's heart.

The Game consists of taking his front paws in hand and wheelbarrowing him backwards down the hill. He must enjoy this, it's all his idea, and still he always looks so *worried* as he dances awkwardly and wincingly away. He is an odd beast, marriage to a human has not been uniformly good for him I think, but he knows just what he wants (like my Will!) and what he wants is this canine wheelbarrow waltz.

"Hey," says Mag suddenly. "I just realized something."

"Go on."

"Here, pick up my feet."

The woman is tinged with madness, so what? I pick up her feet as instructed and she is walking on her hands in the snow, a version of the wheelbarrow waltz that has Felix momentarily confused and yipping. Slightly flighty, reader, but *nimble* at 32, damned nimble to work the waltz in snow like that.

"But what did you realize?" I say.

"Don't you see? When we do it, we have to walk on our front paws, in effect. But Felix hates that, all dogs do. They want to walk on their hind paws."

What she has realized, then, is that dogs and humans differ, obviously a surprise to her on the cognitive level.

"Yet we walk on our hind legs too," I point out. "Look." I refer her to my feet and the fact that I am standing on them.

"Not when we play The Game."

"No. Not when we play The Game."

I guess Mag didn't like feeling peeved with me, our time is short, and so she shifted into her silly mode to yank herself past it and get us back in rhythm. That's all. Now she comes in tighter and wraps both arms around me, making rather a comedy of our forward progress. The rift between us was brief, unwanted, and trivial, so that three minutes later I have completely forgotten it. It never happened. The vast clear snowbound city sleeps below us, every sound is sharp in the crystal acoustic air, and I have begun to feel that magic again. A new departure! New walls, new babies...

Mind you, I have not forgotten Faulkner's advice on the subject of wives, wisdom relayed to you on the first proper page of this narrative, namely to retain at all costs the initial one. And if apt, then doubly apt if you are already working on number two! Faulkner's advice were pithy, reader, it were right pithy, and yet maybe it were also wrong. Or irrelevant. Perhaps it were incomplete. I mean, hey, it is possible to *reject*

The Canine Wheelbarrow Waltz

a pithy wisdom, all things are possible. What about Mickey Rooney, for example. What's he had, something like eight wives? One more than the fellow who was going to St. Ives!

But eight of them, spread out over a 40 year period, a sort of Five Year Plan for rotating the crop. Why not do it that way, a fresh wifelet every five years, it makes a little sense. Confusing for the children? No more so surely than all those hours of TV on Saturday morning. And the truth is it's probably okay, right for some folks and not for some others. More breakthrough thinking: the Rooney Plan for Rooney, the Faulkner Plan for Faulkner!

Now I don't pretend to know the truth about Faulkner or Rooney. Did Faulkner really hang on to the first one? How did that work out for him, all glibness aside? And Rooney. I don't know where he got those eight wives, if it was eight, or where they went. Or how he felt about any of it, as it unfolded. I just divided 8 into 40, though it did seem to work out okay, a wife every five years, why not? It's juke-box gospel, after all, nothing cold as ashes after the fire is gone.

"Maggs," I go, "Did you ever really consider the grand old occupation, housewife and mother? Raising a kid or two, sewing, cooking. I mean, you're so good at all those things, you might be the pluperfect housewife, you might land up someday in the Housewife Hall of Fame."

"Maurice," she goes, "Did you ever, in your occupation as a wordsmith of sorts, notice that 'housewife' may be the most singularly appropriate word in the language? Absolute precision. Housewife: someone who marries a house. I don't want to marry a house, Maurice."

"No." The very thought of marrying a house seems to have aged Maggie, she looks awfully weary in the pale glare of the street lamp.

"It's a trap. It closes on you. I think of my mother."

"There's a good girl."

"Mama was very gay when she was young, she danced and she did some acting. She was poor and full of fun, free, till she met papa. And he didn't do it to her. He was poor and full of fun too."

"So much poverty and fun! And?"

"It just *happens*. Now they're well off and never have any fun at all, as far as I can tell. Mama surely doesn't."

I don't get it yet, but something in it makes me hold my childish tongue for once, and allow her to finish.

"It was probably me and my brothers, as much as anything. She just dried up inside and the years were going by, and now she's this frizzy old lady who throws things at the dinner table and washes the windows every day. Kind of bitter, kind of sentimental. She hates herself, really."

This chilling portrait of Mama Cornelius is sufficiently persuasive; I let the subject of housewiffery drop. It was a distaff novelist who noted that behind every attractive young woman there stands her mother, like a malignant prophecy. Now this truism has been re-stated with such powerful imagery that Maggie is practically aging to bitterness before my eyes, like loose-corked wine.

There is force to it, undeniable force, for I can look back and see that it has indeed just "happened" to all of them, all the mothers of all the attractive young women I have ever known. They were gay and pretty and creative, the world was their oyster, and now they feel cheated and unfulfilled. They did not get their way, only they didn't know it until too late. Tricked! They married houses, all of them.

# FOLDS OF THE HEART

**O**ur hind feet are packed in ice as we turn the last corner and trudge back up to Maggie's door. All the dogs are sleeping now, the bicycle still leans defenseless against the hedge, the standing lamp in the bay window gleams. We wrestle our boots down in the hallway, then quickly put up a pot of chocolate and sit on the floor as close as we can get to the gas ring of the space-heater.

"Nice," Maggie nods, sipping chocolate. Home from the cold, her face is alive with high colors—cheeks in bonny full bloom, forest-green eyes, the roan hair damp and rippling. She could not be more lovely than this.

"Perfect," I say.

"You should have one more cup, though, and get going."

"But not yet! I haven't seen the hunchback. And you wanted me to look at the book too."

"I know I did, but it's late."

I suppose it is, except my watch is set to Freckle Standard Time, or it would be if I had a watch, and so I am prepared to insist it's only three hairs past. So there is time.

I love to wander through Maggie's rooms and poke about her projects, of which there are always ample. Her home is a regular treasure-trove of elaborate undertakings, each of them left lying both *in medias res* and in medias mess. Mag gets most of her living by illustrating children's books and she has spent the day pasting up a section of her latest. Concurrently she has been piecing together a harpsichord kit of demoralizing intricacy and of course she is forever putting the finishing touches on her Hunchback Triptych. The book she does at the kitchen table and it always seems perfectly likely to me that she will paste up the phone bill or a slice of bread by mistake, so jumbled is the prospect. The harpsichord is laid out in Felix' room — yes, you read that right, two of my offspring shared a room for eight years while this furry beast has a room of his own except when harpsichords are being assembled — while the paintings stand on three easels in the studio upstairs, a huge room with six high windows on the southwest side.

Mag's house has always made me think of my garage, although you would have to wonder why (or you would have to wonder why if you knew anything about my garage) for we are discussing a crude hut with a mud floor on the one hand and a six-room duplex with polished red-oak strips on the other. The point of similarity lies here: each place makes a perfect example of that neglected genre, the environmental self-portrait, each place is a personality in the outward shape of a house or habitation.

I rented the garage to live in many years ago, in college it was, before I met Adele Blaney. It was dirt cheap (Hell, it was dirt) and it seemed to be All I Needed. Rude and small, it held certain advantages for someone a slob and poor. I could heat it and light it for practically nothing with kerosene, and it seemed not only complete but also to me aesthetically superior to many of the larger, nicer homes I saw. It suited. There were those who disliked a dirt floor and laughed to see me outside ditching the perimeter during a heavy rainstorm, and yet what better surface really for a young man with two dogs to board and an old Indian motorcycle that dripped oil? I came and I went, wrote silly poems and picked my 5-string, and tuned the Indian twice a week — possibly my happiest time.

It is so much easier to take a small place alone, if you would seek to make it perfect. So easy, by analogy, to write a perfect word. Watch me: River. Steel. Lamentation. Hobo. Lupine. Harmonium. Even a perfect phrase, a sentence. Paragraphs are manageable, whole pages and stories possible, but how many large entire books can have been perfect? A matter of taste, surely, as with houses, but let us agree few or none. One often hears that *Anna Karenina* is a perfect book, but it is not despite its irrefutable greatness. (See my "The Long Flight to Astapovo" for more on this.) Clearly the more you take on, the more you invite imperfection, though of course perfection may well be a sterile useless aim in the first place.

Still it is interesting to have every square inch of what you call your "space" just exactly as you want it, everything in its place and totally pleasing so that your scantling life is itself a work of art. Maggie's house is just such a self-portrait, though you could hardly do the six-room self-portrait without you were a certain sort of person. The sort who has salvage furniture and slovenly closets, transient animals and a high threshold for disrepair. Also odd precious objects, beloved slants of light, stacks of scratched recordings, ludicrously balanced tiers of books and old photographs, and the familiar discontinuous crockery, no two cups or plates too closely resembling one another in size or design. It isn't for everyone, reader, whirl is king here, but it is Maggie, and there is a strong whiff of home to it all.

It makes me miss my garage and the simple joy of unsummoned youth I could count on there. To live alone in the bee-loud glade! Maybe I should have stayed there, or kept it at least for a secret hideout. Really it cost me less to rent it for the year than it would cost me now to meet Kim for lunch downtown. It was a place, that's all it was, but a room of one's own — even Felix seems to need one. I think about kids and their rooms, myself as a kid, Will, Sadie, Ben. In that room a kid will know exactly how it all lays out, where each and every blessed object can be found, cause he put it there and that's where he wants it to be. Don't ask him to tidy up, it *is* tidy. It may look upside down and backwards to you, but it is in absolute rational order to him.

When do we outgrow the need for such sanctuary, at what point do we start preferring to share it? When we head off to school, or to the army, and have "mates"? Room-mates, or bunk-mates, eventually mate-mates for most of us, little spousies? That is when we lose it, reader, but at what point did we cease to prefer it, or outgrow our need of it? Never. We never did. We need it still! In Benny's room, he knows, is his "stuff". In my garage was my stuff. Maggie's duplex, Maggie's stuff. It's why she's happy.

Meanwhile we are up in her workroom, the room that shamed all other real estate when she hunted house, for through this bank of tall French windows there flows more and better daylight than one finds in the early Renaissance panoramas of Heaven. Come to Rockland Terrace and you will soon enough put by the old saw about north light for a painter's studio. Here the defining light pours steadily from the southwest most of the day and by it Mag has painted the three large canvasses we are now viewing, the Triptych.

The Hunchback Triptych is my name for these paintings by the way, not Maggie's, and I call them that because that is what they amount to, three different portraits of the same hunchbacked man. On the left, currently, he is grasping a safety strap on the subway car while eating an apple. The middle panel shows him crossing a street, among taller straighter people. And the one on the right has him seated on a green park bench, not eating his lunch but balancing it on his lap. This one, which I call "Hunchback with Lunchbox", Maggie calls "Sitting".

These pictures somehow mix the rawness of naturalism with the boldness of poster art and as compositions they make powerful affecting views of the gentleman in question. A lot of the power comes of his hunch, or humph, although I gather that to Mag the whole point is to make him perfectly ordinary. He is a man, not a hunchback. Not even a man who is also a hunchback; a man. I did a similar thing once, actually, wrote a story in which one of the two characters was Negro, only I never said so, I didn't describe him as such. I knew he was black, of course, but anyone reading the thing could hardly be expected to guess at the fact. Too cute by half, reader, I gave a party and no one came. Really I gave a party and no one was even invited to come. My smug little gambit was so subtle it didn't exist, in practical terms. With a painting, of course, you would have the exact opposite problem, what you paint *shows* and so a hunch is a hunch is a hunch.

At the moment, however, I am not seeing lunch-backs or hunch-boxes up there, I am not seeing the paintings at all. I am peering out of the corner of my soul and seeing Maggie Cornelius, her lips slightly compressed, as she awaits my worthless assessment of her work. I have always been more in touch with my need for Maggie than with any clear notion of her need for me and yet at this moment, for the first time, I can feel it the other way. Just this second it seems the air might go out of her, that she might sag, and it fills me with new wonder.

There are so many new questions I would like to ask her, had I only the momentum of phrasing to begin, a context. For starters, did she honestly never have that empty sensation of filling life up rather than it was full? Like reading bad books with that filthy I'm-reading-this-to-pass-the-time feeling, or watching TV compulsively when you knew the shows were perfectly dreadful? You looked at them to get to eleven o'clock, to bed-time, but then it felt so sickening, so desperate

and clearly defeating to have endured the stuff passively—like
eating potato chips for dinner, nauseous and empty when you
finish...

"You've changed it," I say, a flat damp attempt to idle for
time while I chase after this freight-train of thought.

"Not very much."

"No, it's subtle. It's that little splash of silver on the lunchbox. Am I right?"

"It sticks out like a sore thumb, doesn't it? It stinks."

Mag looks miserable, to me anyway, at this moment. Am I
seeing straight, or blurry? Her hazel eyes, so recently sharp
and green, now brown as mud? Is it just an accident of
lighting that makes her look like nothing so much as a friend
in need? I want to help and I want to ask. About all those hot
baths and cold dinners and the sixty pages per night of a good
Martian novel so you could tell yourself and your liked-ones
that at least you were reading the Martians...

"No, it's the right idea, Mag. Maybe just mute it a shade."

She nods, but she is only humoring me back and in so doing
dismisses the moment before I can manage to grasp or define
it, all my half-formulated questions still wholly unspoken. She
comes in for a landing now, stands on my feet and presses her
nose to mine so that I am forced to either cross my eyes or
shut them. And thus softly takes charge.

"You really should go, my friend. It's after one o'clock."

"I know, but I'm not going."

"What do you mean?"

"I mean I'm not going. I'm staying."

"You're not even *invited* to stay," she insists, to save me
from myself, in case I'm not kidding. I am and I am not. I
won't stay the night, but we have important business yet to
transact, I feel sure of it.

"We've hardly had a chance to talk," I say. "A quick fuck, a
walk, and out?"

"Two sustained fucks, a fine leisurely stroll, the Grand Tour, and out. You shouldn't be silly, Maurice. Won't Kim have been worrying already? You have never been this late."

"Kim doesn't believe in worrying and in any case she's probably sound asleep. I want to talk to you."

Mag has guided me down the stairs by now to the foyer where she catches her breath and holds it in consideration. She may want to protect me from myself, then again she may simply want to protect herself from me. If she is indeed a friend in need, does she need me to stay or to leave? Her hesitation at any rate concludes in a smile, and she tugs me to her.

"Well, let's lie down, then," she says, and we turn back onto the staircase together, slowly, like partners in a minuet. Somehow on the way up, though, clothes begin to come off us and the clothes are getting left on the stairs. It takes a while to surmount the staircase because we are suddenly giddy, laughing and grappling with the clothes. We end up naked on the top landing and couple at once, so simply.

"I can't do this," I say, "I'm 40 years old."

"There *is* something wrong with us tonight," Maggie laughs, and if it is true we seem especially itchy tonight, it is also true that this is the first verbal interchange in the history of our sex life, the sole occasion I can recall on which we were conjoined yet then conversed. Once underway, however, we continue along with surprising fluency.

"What did you lace that chocolate with, anyway?"

"You really must go now, Maurice," Maggie deadpans.

"I know, I really must, and then you'll have me coming and going. But what was it? We can package it, our fortune will be made..."

Oh we are rolling easy at this point, so comfortably lulled by the dull ache of pleasure that it seems we might go on for days this way without conclusion, basking in a richly

On the Stair-landing

amplified sensitivity that our earlier efforts have earned us. We are threatened only by the dog, for Felix when not properly constrained by doors does often seek to join us at times like this, his timing is generally impeccable, and in the back of my mind I have begun to expect him momentarily on the back of my body.

"How's your back?" I ask, on the subject of backs, as Maggie's is halfway on a scratchy little scrap of rug and half on the hardwood landing.

"Finethankyou," she reports dreamily. I can tell she is in the same shape as I am, feathered edges of the brain, sliding down below the waves of nectar toward unconsciousness, close to the unpleasant oversensitivity of the post-orgasmic shiver. I figure if we keep on talking to each other, we will at least avert the danger of lapsing into coma, however sweet.

"Mag?"

"Yeh?"

"Are you sure we shouldn't consider a life together?"

"Nuh," she murmurs absently, "not sure." Perhaps I ought to say that we have never really discussed this issue before, it has never even been raised, and in truth I have always assumed that on Maggie's part this was out of consideration for me. Keeping to the original sporting bargain, not rocking the boat once it's been launched and all. But here she stops me good and solid. Still dreamy, mind you: "But pretty sure."

Is this an example of coherent thought? She has heard the question and understood it, answered fully and accurately?

"What do you mean?" I say, not smoothly, I fear.

"What do *you* mean?" she says. Her eyes are still closed, mine are open. She is still moving, I think I am not.

"Oh, well, I meant just us, you and me."

"That sort of us."

"Yes."

"That's what I thought you meant." Now her eyes are open too. "Hey, where are you going? Don't go away."

Maggie has me clamped inside her strong thighs and she holds on while I start to sort matters out and try to find a perspective. I hadn't really meant anything, you understand, I was just talking with my mouth. If I had been thinking at all, I would have thought about Mama Cornelius winding up to toss the gravy-boat, or of Kim Orenburg, or at the very least of Maggie herself, the sanctity and sanity of her life alone. But my mouth made an utterance that created a disturbance, and hers made a reply, and now I find I'm hit!

Nor is it Maggie's style to mitigate a home-shot, to qualify or clarify, or to reduce a sentence out of mere mercy. She's not hard exactly but she is dangerously honest, gives what she gives, no more no less, and lets the chips fall where they may. I have always respected and honored this approach, and have found it almost unique in her. No inclination to fluff it up, no false or hyperflated endearments; never will she say the words "I love you" (I'm almost certain she has a principle against it) and still I must confess to you that I have believed she loves me, and furthermore that given the chance she would be glad to have me more of the time, in a more proper format. To hear the reverse from her now is, well, an unpleasant shock, bit of an ice-bath, really.

"Why are you so sure?" I manage.

"I said I was not sure. *Pretty* sure."

"Why are you pretty sure, then?"

"You know."

"I don't, though. It's all right, tell me."

She won't, of course. I get the feeling that Maggie wants to speak, that she would break precedent and explain herself to me, but that she literally *can't*, as a fish can't fly. Or better, as a child can never respond to the deceptive question, "Why did you do that?"

She does kiss my face, most tenderly, and this is to let me know she holds great affection, I should not doubt she holds the greatest affection for me. I do know full well she espouses a cynical worldly line on relationships, I have heard her state that every day on the surface of the earth one million couples who have exchanged the vow to love forever, will dissolve forever instead. And from my own experience I know the jist of this is true and that the truth in it is pause-giving indeed. Still, in the gut, in the soil of the gut where no self-deception takes seed, I have assumed she would be happy with me if I were only free for her.

Only once, shortly after Capistrano, has my conviction in this been shaken. We had rarely mentioned the future, the territory ahead, and when we had it did seem our talking faltered immediately, like an engine badly tuned. But on that one occasion I was slightly carried away, to the extent of picturing a few of the pleasures we might look forward to in winter, I and Maggie, and even making casual reference to that admittedly uncharted yet presumably inevitable time. And Maggie looked up as though I had just shot her in the leg and was waiting to hear how she had liked it.

"After Christmas!" she said. "I may not even be here after Christmas. You may not be here."

"I'll be here," I replied. "Where would you be?"

"Wherever. Things come up."

"What things? Where would you go?"

"Anywhere. Back to Scotland. The Black Sea, the Swiss Alps, the Florida Keys... It's a big world, Maurice."

"I forgot it was so big," I had to admit, and as you know I really *have* forgotten that fact. Also the fact that Maggie wasn't mine, she was hers. What I wanted to say, of course, and naturally didn't, was "What about *me*?"

Instead she said something dumb about despair, how despair was impossible because the world was so big, and I nodded in dumb agreement, fronting only a vest-pocket version of despair, a tiny explosion in my face, that would wash off later. But here, months later, was a significantly larger charge, more powder in the sack, and it has reached the high ground of fortification we have staked out together since that distant October day.

And so too, here I am—on a day to question the very essence of domesticity, to worry the process by which a man chooses to make himself so accountable, to research the possibility (or impossibility) of being a different character altogether—and I find that Maggie Cornelius *is* that character!

It is hard to clarify the matter, because Maggie is a genuinely sweet and deeply affectionate woman who at the same time does carry a grain of coldness in her breast, a strain of apartness. Is it the mistrust of others, or is it strictly in and of herself? Is she this way because she cannot see settling down, or can she not see settling down because she is this way? I have experienced the many small forms of this barrier she puts up between us and have been close to her in spite of it. It has not seemed to me an essential barrier, like the absence of empathy or attraction, but merely a detail of personality, and a strength after all.

Indeed it is no joke that I see in her the very being I thought of becoming earlier this evening at Bourbon-on-the-Charles; the me that might have stayed in my garage, with two dogs and a motorcycle, in 1959; the me that might have reached the great grey-green greasy Limpopo River, and befriended the bi-coloured python rock-snake. She has love in her heart, nothing could be clearer to me, and yet she gives it only so much leverage over the rest of her, and no more. The rest of her, then, vaster than her love!

Meanwhile I am, or have been on the verge of asking Maggie if she wishes to "call it off" between us, but somehow I find the sense to hang fire, the strength to suppress my undignified pride. I know the answer and so I know I would only be asking out of self-pity, fishing for reassurance. They say you can knock forever on a dead man's door and I say you can fish forever for reassurance at Maggie's—it is one thing she simply cannot give. Can't give verbally, that is, for as I say she is holding on tight and I know if I open my eyes again she will be looking right into them with that soft loving frown of hers, the one that clearly expresses the love she will never recite.

She wants nothing from me, she likes our liaison exactly as we have defined it. From one angle of vision our situation remains that Maggie is free and I am bound by marriage and family; from another, that I am free and she is bound by commitments to herself. No matter what I may want, she will refuse to make an honest man of me, as it were, so that if I happened to be a woman it could be said I was being "used" and used badly. Nota bene, Sadie Locksley! But even now I cannot remotely feel this, for Mag's strategy has already taken effect, the strategy whereby she simply waits while I founder in the wake of a particularly nasty or painful truth.

Certainly I must rise to the challenge, for it is after all a test of my strength and imagination both, this casting about for perspective. And I also can't help feeling excited by it, by the sheer table-turning surprise of it, and excited most keenly by the thrill of seeing my alter ego in ascendancy, depicting for me my alter existence. But no one has spoken for quite a time and it is plain enough that any joy or vitality we felt before, in the precise posture we still occupy (known as the "missionary" position in your guide to extant Somerville stair-landings) has been effortlessly transformed into a hapless tension and distance between us. This is a uniquely human bungle, to search out moments of high pleasure and convert them into self-induced pain, by too carefully examining every "fold of the heart".

So we were sailing high, miles above the city, like Peter Pan and Wendy gone randy, and now instead we have begun to feel acute discomfort at the elbows, the knees... "Tell me," I had said, and not a word from either since, though I have been working my way back toward Maggie the whole while, valuing her honesty and admiring her resolve to remain within her metaphorical garage, strewn with her own personal litter, rich with the scent of her cooking, turned smoothly to the shape of her will. Working my way toward treating her at this moment just as I would wish her to treat me, had I been the one with courage; not to punish her for it, not a punishable offense, and furthermore she has taken the pain of it onto herself, she has made the decision. I have faced such choices many times, tonight and long ago, and I have found them to be excruciating, not to say impossible. Better sometimes to be crushed quickly by fate than crumbled slowly by the doubt and indecision of years.

"Hey," says Maggie at last, speaking in the gentle voice one might use in addressing a sleepy child. I have been groping after an opening of my own, some word or two not too false, if only to remove the burden from her, but now it is too late, she has taken that on too. "Hey. You falling asleep?"

"No, I'm here." I speak gently too. My gentlest nonjudgmentalist "No, I'm here."

"It's past two."

"No! Must run." She still has me in the old scissors hold and grins as I perform a pantomime of futile running, a brief skit of exaggerated helplessness. "Must run. Can't."

"Maurice," she says, her face abruptly serious. "Maybe you should tell Kim the truth tonight. Maybe that would make things easier all around."

It must be that I look, as she did herself not so very long ago, a bit pinched about the smile, like a friend in need. We're just trying to help each other out tonight, I and Maggie, taking turns at it.

"Tell Kim? Oh sure, good, I'll tell her."

"Seriously, though."

Well seriously, there are two points to consider here. The first is that Mag is not totally insincere. She may be so non-possessive herself that she truly cannot fathom the extent to which a person can be uncontrollably discharged from reason by jealousy. She may truly assume that a right-thinking woman like Kim Orenburg, whose poetry she has admired, would never demean herself by obstructing such a fine and frankly benign rapport as I and Maggie happen to share. The claims of monogamy are as crude and ill-drawn to her as the claims of ethnic prejudice, merely ideas that are in the ascendancy but wrong.

The second point to consider, though, is that Mag is not altogether sincere either. For she knows, from me, that Lady Orenburg did once belabor my brain-pan with a banjo and moreover that her motive in this barbaric display lay in my lying alongside a woman other than herself, lying tangent to be precise, in attitudes of affection and hopefully pleasure. And so the real meaning of Mag's suggestion is strictly between the two of us, and solely for my benefit, a re-statement of our very existence. If there is something to tell Kim, why then there *is something*: we exist because we confess. As much as to say, Yes, we are still going strong, there is a future for us, but we must continue to speak of that future only in the present tense.

Meantime I am pulling on my boots, heavily dressed while Maggie remains on the top stair still naked, pensively hugging her knees. The auburn hair streams wild and lovely, and frames the quiet contrasting beauty of her softest eyes and lips.

"It would make things easier," I say. "Much easier. She'll be tickled pink, in fact. She'll pack nice snacks for us, I bet, she'll want to. She'll write us love poems, sonnets, in the second person plural and *she* will fetch the beer and toaste."

"You aren't giving her credit. She's not an idiot."

Excellent point, and well taken. Kim is hardly an idiot. And therefore it is possible she already knows about Maggie Cornelius and has just been waiting for me to buy a new banjo. Indeed there is no taking her for granted either—she may be spending her afternoons in bed with another man. She may know about Maggie and have taken a lover. She may *not* know about Maggie and have taken three lovers! Why assume otherwise?

"I'm going to be tired tomorrow," I say.

"Sleep late."

"Ben," I reply.

Mag has pulled a cotton robe around her now and is knotting the waistband. This is preparatory to escorting me outside, for our traditional last kiss through the rolled-down window of the car. I am pushing her back inside the house, or trying to, because she has bare feet and it is 15 degrees Fahrenheit out here. From somewhere down the block Felix materializes, sprinting toward us like Rin-Tin-Tin on dexedrine, and crashes against me hoping to initiate The Game.

"What will you tell her, if you tell her?" says Maggie.

"I won't tell her, unless she asks."

"What will you tell her if she asks, then?"

I shrug. "The truth."

And that's as far as Maggie takes it. What "the truth" is neither of us knows at this point, though we are both aware of the specific crimes it subsumes. Surprising enough she asked. Maybe she would want to blow it all up, to have me or have done with me, though I can't honestly say I believe it. But she has asked an uncharacteristic question, made a light passing probe into the none-of-Maggie's-business file (as filed by Maggie) and she will not now pursue it to uncharacteristic lengths.

"Call me tomorrow?" she says.

"Sure, if you like." Maggie generally feels about time spent on the telephone as I do about time spent with the dental hygienist.

"We messed it up a little tonight," she explains. "It'll be better if we can just say hello tomorrow. I'll be home all day."

"Sure. Now get inside."

"I want to go once around the block with Felix," she says, blowing me an extra kiss. She is running in place now, her own comic pantomime, and the dog is primed to burst forward with her first stride. She pivots, he bursts, and they're off. Maggie in her flimsy, flopping cotton robe and bare feet, her mama would spank her for sure. Or maybe fling something at her.

"Madman!" I cry after. She stops and faces me, smiling.

"Don't forget to call me, I want you to."

"*Well* then," I say with hollow ironic intent, but Maggie has already sprinted away, knees pumping high against the hardening snow, down the hill half-naked like a nightmare of flight, sweet dream of freedom.

## PHOEBE ISN'T DEAD

O f course I have no call feeling rejected in the matter of I and Maggie. I have been accepted absolutely. Granted it was a 5-star shockeroo when moments ago she said, so softly, "Pretty sure" to my question and yet from Maggie there was a shade of tribute in the qualifying adjective; not sure but "pretty sure". Over the past 15 years she has been asked the question often, and I have reason to suspect she has not often found use for the qualifying adjective. Mag does want and need me, and in just the way our original bargain was struck. *I'm* the one rocking the boat.

Imagine: a woman of extraordinary charms, a woman who on first sight stops you in your tracks like a high calibre bullet, takes you as her lover on your terms—she takes you and she leaves you be! No harping at you to abandon the wife, no pressing after declarations or tokens of overvalued stone; simply enjoying you when you show up, kissing you an unsentimental farewell, and enjoying you again next time you manage to appear. It is nothing less than fantasy made real, paterfamilias' dream fulfilled.

So why this clutching reflex? That is what it is, you see, literally a reflex. One does not decide to require devotion, nor does one decide against requiring it. It is not a matter for reflection, but rather for reflexion. And so often we clutch and grab and whine until at last we have acquired devotion at

the awful cost of crushing whatever affection once lay behind
it. I and Maggie are decent folk, this is an honest love affair —
why deface it with charmless demands, like some heavily
armed terrorist of the heart? Fear of loss, that's why.

I have after all tried to "eliminate" Maggie and I'll tell you
the closest I've come to date. I worked out a little game in
which I imagined how the different members of my family
might see Maggie, to let *them* place her for me, at least
hypothetically. Kim I guessed would try to see her as false and
thwarted, sort of a glorified hippie or worse, a phony glorified
hippie. Would be unable to overlook the discipline, however,
or the obvious charm both artistic and personal, and so would
struggle through to an admiration without trust. Speaking
from her own experience, Kim would say, Yes, all this is
good, but wouldn't you trade it for love if you had the chance,
love with all its nasty baggage?

Benny's my empirical study, he has met her, and he was
bowled over along with the other short-stops at Sleepy
Hollow Daycare. He would stick with her too, as he stands by
all his first impressions. And Sadie would agree she was a
"wicked neat" lady; they'd be friends and if Maggie advised
her to pass up the Prom, she'd pass it up proudly. She might
even make Maggie's house an after-school hang-out, were it
not for the distance. But Will. There's the rub. I think
Willie's guidance counselor, not to say his mother, would be
surprised how little that kid misses. He really does see the
whole floor. To me he is the truly human litmus test, the
proof, and I strongly suspect he would wish Maggie warmer.
He would never insist, or criticize, but something subtle in his
face would say he wished he could find her warmer.

And that's the closest I've come. It might be close enough,
mind you, if Maggie wasn't in my blood a bit by now. I could
spend an evening at the gym each week (maybe take Will
along!) and I could restore lapsed friendships — sit in at

Macauley's for poker, or at Bernstein's for beer and big-screen hockey... When it has gone to the blood, though, there's no real way to fight it. A man can aim to live right and be rewarded for so doing with a rich profound unhappiness that pervades the very senses through which he would perceive the world. Everywhere at once the lights of this world go dimmer, the wind backs down from our hollow sails. Kim v. Maggie, no problem, but Heart v. Head, head and heart in disharmony, that can push a man around. And like a little devil-engine of literally internal combustion it can also cause him to push others around, innocent third parties, loved ones. The behavior turns strange.

Weekend before last, for instance, I woke on Saturday from a dream of Capistrano and proceeded to act relentlessly inhuman to my wife and child all day. Over breakfast, where a desperate third cup of oil-black coffee failed to lift my melancholia or tune down my howling head-ache; at the Franklin Park Zoo, God help me, where I inexplicably denied my son ice cream as an unconscious penalty for his beautiful existence; at friends' later that evening, where I sniped venomously at every individual and institution and ended by insulting my hosts, their food, their music, the very raiment that hid their perfections and their imperfections, and all for what?

For no better reason, no *other* reason, than my too keen awareness of Maggie Cornelius, for with all the pleasures I was blessed with that day I could, in my triviality and ingratitude, imagine surpassing pleasures. Maggie had planned "nothing special" that weekend and if she followed through on her plan, which in my triviality and ingratitude I could hope she had, then how perfectly maddening I could not do "nothing special" with her, thereby making it special, as are all the mundane objective correlatives of the heart's eternal return.

There was no sleep for me that night, no relief the next day. Here I was in the bosom of my extended nuclear family, all five of us skating on the swan-boat pond at Boston Gardens under a Sunday blue sky; here was Benny gleefully pursuing Will around-about the island in the pond and Sadie intently rehearsing her backward eights; here was my bride, gliding toward me with a grin and a jug of the cheap red inside her coat. And in the midst of this picture-perfect Americana, this Norman Rockwell moment in my life, I was perfectly joyless, nervous and irritable. My mind was elsewhere, only my resentments were here.

It is hard to believe or understand as I write it down now, that the plainness of Maggie's back-porch could pull me away from my portion of winter paradise, but I remember very clearly that it felt that way at the time, and when it feels that way, when it takes and pushes me around, I can be bad, consummately bad against all my will and judgment. It stinks, it makes me feel like an insect, but there it is all the same. Because, you see, it's just fine to descry the folly of starting over, again, and yet one need not underwrite the Rooney Plan as such to perceive that it would be simply insupportable to bear passive witness or give tacit consent to the departure of Maggie Cornelius for the vales of Scotland, or any of those groovy tourist meccas she cited as being part of this big world of possibilities that makes despair so impossible.

Oh dear oh dear, je suis conflicted and in most sadly conventional manner I fear, and yet you must trust my veracity when I tell you that at this moment the conflict which I have only just finished tediously elaborating and which does indeed sit at the epicenter of the tale I am both telling and living tonight, that selfsame conflict has glanced off me like a dash of sunlight off some fast-moving chrome. There are many things on my mind as I drive, poor bedraggled mind to be sure, but though vital matters abound the trivial is foremost, namely, what explanation do I offer for arriving Locksley Hall at this ungodly hour on an occasion when Kim has specifically urged me to hurry home as early as possible? And what explanation indeed, if I am determined not to lie! None of your flat tires, your wet spark-plugs, busted hoses and gas-line freezes, not even a wrong turn in the blinding blizzard leading me 47 miles out of my way, 94 round-trip, all the way to Boxboro and back...

People determine to be honest for different reasons, not the least being that honesty does often make the best web of deceit. They say if you tell the truth you don't have to remember what you said, in order to avoid contradicting it six months later. Trouble is my memory is so bad that I can tell the best truth I know and contradict myself anyway! So with me it's more a question of principle, this truth thing, although I am by no means a narrow constructionist in the matter.

For example I could stop at a tavern and drink "some beer", then on to the Hall to report that I had stopped at a tavern to drink "some beer". Snowy night, caught a mood, passed a speck of time in a clean well-lighted place. Plenty of witnesses to that, surely, except we have a slight practical problem here. This is Boston, not New York or San Francisco, so all the liquories are long since locked. Bourbon-on-the-Charles is dark, the tradesmen are all in their bunks snoring like chainsaws.

But you get the idea. Such an account may seem cynical to you, incomplete or misleading, and hopefully it is. Yet it is not a lie. It is a deception, part art and part cheat, but with a basis in fact that leaves the deceived a fair chance at uncovery. Holmes would see through. Whereas in the instance of an outright lie, the internal evidence, however imaginative or for that matter convincing, is at bottom false. Only independent evidence can prevail against it, Holmes must make his field investigation. The lie then misleads as to fact, the deception only as to meaning. See the D.?

Again. Had I and Maggie done all our love-making there on the stair-landing, I could report that I had run into a woman who was stuck in the snow (she had got sort of stuck at one point on our walk) and had taken her home, a woman I had met once at Benny's day-care (true true) and we had done some talking (indeed!) and No! we had certainly *not* gone to bed together. Alas, we did not do all our love-making there on the stair-landing, to bed together we had gone, and so gone too is that particular option. Next:

But no. No next. I have real problems, lots of 'em, and here I am lavishing whatever mental energy I have left on the piddling matter of ill-timed arrivals. Why bother? Why sneak in there aswarm with gnats of guilt, why even consider apologizing for anything, much less for being human, at the age of 40? I'm halfway to the barn, reader, can't I be my self yet? Can't I just go to the kitchen for a brownie and two sips of milk, go to the bathroom to splash cold water on my face and polish my choppers, go to bed and sleep? No doubt I could slide past the whole business anyway with a joke and a groan of fatigue—sorry I was gone so long, luv, just took a leisurely lunch, groan of fatigue, snore snore. There is the morning, yes, but there is also gentle Ben in the morning and I invite you to recall that the record for consecutive sentences completed, in English by a holding parent, is two. It would take more than two consecutive sentences, I should hope, to ferret out a Locksley omission!

Clearly the best plan is no plan at all, too tired and wrassled to make a plan, better just to wing it. So I leave off considering and I am back under the wheel, rolling over the loose-packed snow at an hour when the streets are literally empty. (The whole way from Union Square to the river I will see nothing moving.) In Union Square there are decorations, big tin Santas and reindeer flapping from the light stanchions, beribboned wreaths draped over the police emergency call-boxes. Some of the shop windows are frosted with glitter or sprayed white and stencilled: Season's Greetings.

You have to wonder about Christmas—did Christ really go to the discount store with his Visa card for you and for me?—but the truth is I remain moved by the holiday season, cheered at its approach, dejected by its inevitable disappointments. I don't mean that Santa fails to bring me the right stuff, the stuff I so painstakingly list in my annual letter to the North Pole. I mean that a season of hope begets a season of despair, just that. There's despair in the air around Christmas-time, lots of it, clinging to every mistletoe and bright-wrapped gift, the clichés come home to roost at Christmas. It's a time for reaping whirlwinds and yes, a staging-ground for all our grudges and guilt. Good old guilt.

I found a sadness at Adele's house tonight, something was missing. Was it me? Would there be something sad out there if I had helped to trim the tree? If my shoes were in the closet next Adele's, and the two of us sat down in the kitchen each with our section of the newspaper? Could such a slight increase in the population at West dispel the sadness, an increase of one? But this is no good, Locksley, who's fooling who. There's no place for glibness in the interior monologue, you are only being glib with your self. "Slight increases in the population" are not the natural converse of broken homes. You may think it's swell to rib Willie for ten minutes, shoot 2 for 2 from the floor, and get away with something, but no one is fooled by such callow short-changing. Will knows. And you know he'd rather you went 9 for 46 from the floor, if you see what I mean, which you do, you and I in this particular sentence both being me. (Hello, Locksley here!)

Along the riverway I do see an occasional car, Honk if you love Jesus, Pendergast for Sheriff. Here the moon-pierced clarity of the sky is suffused with emissions from the Giants of Pollution, slightly surreptitious nocturnal dispensations of sulphur gas and carbon compounds to the slumbering public. At no extra charge? Nonsense, you are dreaming, it costs big money to pollute! I wind inland from the widening Charles and what a marvel it is to navigate these streets alone, outnumbered two to one by police cruisers (a *good* ratio for citizen safety) and with none of those maddening red lights, just the friendly wink of orange all the way to Fennel Alley.

Home. A naked sensation, defenselessness, as I spin the key to gain the Hall. It comes of not knowing where one stands. To gird the loins for battle or to gird them simply for bed, that is the question. Distinctly possible there is no battle needs fighting here and yet unenlightened I am like the prisoner of war who has been listed dead in action for six years, returning to his suburban home more fearful of meeting his successor than joyful at the anticipation of his wife's embrace. The not-knowing catches me up, in the hall mirror my face looks confused. Is that me? I growl, it growls; me.

In the kitchen I find evidence that at last consciousness Kim Orenburg must still have valued my friendship. There is a note on the counter, a manila sheet folded once over, and atop it, yes, a brownie. As advertised, then, the brownie and the two sips of milk! Overcome with famine at the sight of the tidy cakelet, I slide it in entire, four cubic inches at a single bite, and then unfold the note. Sandbagged:

> M. I bet you one
> dollar you have
> already gorfed up the
> brownie. (Place dollar
> under sugar bowl.
> Thank you.)      K.

Kim seems to feel I'm a chozza for sweets, and she's been campaigning to have my mouth declared a lethal weapon by the courts. But the brownie has indeed been consumed, so in the interests of fair play I slip a bill underneath the sugar bowl before looking in on her. She is sleeping, in the odd familiar array. One leg juts up and out from under the covers, angled at the knee and exposed right up to the sleek curve which though now continuous will divide into buttock and thigh whenever she straightens the leg. And despite the hour, and my bone-deep fatigue, despite any activities essayed earlier in the company of Mlle. Cornelius, I wish to touch this leg, to stroke it. I am become a beast, it seems, and yet there she is, so lovely in the play of moonlight on the careless flannel sheets, the dark curls falling across her mouth. And I can feel nothing like guilt because I know I love her.

But wait, I don't believe we were discussing guilt, we were eating cake and admiring the wife. And I don't *feel* guilt, I feel innocence, very deeply in fact, except...Except I have felt guilt for Willie, dammit, for Sadie and for that sadness. Never exactly *not* felt it, because guilt is a quiet plague, it's odorless and colorless and it blends with the very air we breathe until it's just another element, like nitrogen or oxygen. I've been snorting it all night—why deny it?—and it's a great low, man, but I think I've just seen through it, man, and I want to let it go, cold Christmas turkey. Cause in the meandering delirium of this full moon morning, with inspiration drawn from the Orenburg haunch, I have just unearthed a fragment from my own childhood, and the meaning of that fragment has instantly permeated my parenthood, my husbandhood, my very sweatshirt hood! Let me tell it.

I was six years old and my father had taken me to watch of all things a golf match at a country club. This was, or was somehow made to seem, a big deal. Money was involved and broadcasters were there and to me it was pretty exciting, like the circus or a parade. We were gathered behind a single strand of rope at the final green and the contending players, in a foursome, were lining up their approach shots. One landed a few feet from the flag and the crowd erupted in whistles and cheers. My father gave me a nudge and said it was a great shot. The next ball sailed past the flag, skipped once, and rolled right toward us, came rolling right under the strand of rope at the edge of the crowd.

Now I had seen a baseball game or two, and I was aware that the big thing for a kid was the foul ball hit into the stands, a ball up for grabs, a souvenir. It never crossed my mind the game of golf might be different and so I never guessed there was any mischief in it—the ball was ours. I scooped it in and smiled up at my pa. I can still see him, head back and laughing, just before all hell broke loose. Everyone started shouting and shoving, hundreds of them pointing their angry faces at me, and I simply bolted. Clutching the ball, I scrambled through a sand-trap, up over a hill, and into the pine woods beyond. And my father ran with me. Laughed and ran and went prone with me in the forest, just as though we were a pair of owl-hoots salting away the strong-box from the Dodge City stage-coach haul.

My father was a humble man who ran the hardware in our town and who therefore owed much to the good will of his fellow townspeople. It could not pay him to appear any too fun-loving or unreliable, and though I may not have fully understood it at the time, his dash with me that summer day showed a rare instinct. For sure he might just as well have tripped me, slapped me till I coughed up the ball, and stopped my allowance for the rest of the month. But he ran with me instead. And though the record may show him less than perfect, may reveal that he liked a bottle and wandered a bit in the night (and for all I know he may have been swimming in whiskey that afternoon at the country club), all those sins and omissions come to nothing alongside the one shining moment of true and perfect fatherhood. For goodness is real, love is real, and it easily outweighs the mistakes and peccadillos of our quotidian history.

Have I been as much to Will? I hope so. I have stood with him and laughed, never have I taken sides against him. I have loved him every moment in my heart, literally every moment, and knowing it I feel ready to kick the habit, I feel safe. I feel I could be in a roomful of people all snorting clean uncut Dusseldorf and not take a hit of guilt, though I suppose I'm only kidding myself along. I suppose the physics of this epiphany will pass, or my affect for it will fade, and guilt will have its innings again. You can run, gentle reader, but you can't hide. I'm almost afraid to change my stance or my angle of vision, for it was this particular prospect of Kim asprawl that brought forth memory and sentiment alike.

So cancel the epiphany if you must, hold the mayo, and let's just enjoy the relief while it lasts. Because it *is* true, you owe them your love, you can't owe them your life entire, and I believe Willie knows. Knows me and knows my love for him. As the late Davy Crockett was fond of saying, "Fais ce que doit, advienne que pourra!" Or words to that effect.

I wish Will was with us tonight, so I could look at him right now, touch his face. Ben is in there, of course, and I visit him instead, bearing silent witness to his peaceful slumbers. Do you by any chance know the movie, a comedy with Jason Robards playing a philanderer who whenever pressured by mistress Jane Fonda to abandon his wife and family, can always reduce the lady to tears and sympathy instead by conjuring up the image of his happy unsuspecting children with their soft dreamy faces and their "little arms flung up over their little heads"? I have seen Will and Sadie in their innocence, arms flung up that way, and I see Benny now, and it is not a joke, even if it was one in the movie. They are touching at such times, laid open, unhurt and trusting...

But that sadness out at Adele's house, I think I know what it is now, and it isn't coming from Adele or the kids or the season or even good old guilt, really. It's coming from me, part and parcel of my mid-life crisis. It's the greasy underbelly of the emotion du jour, the flip side of my lively evening—it's my death. Because death doesn't come to you all at once, you know, with the kiss of a truck, it usually occurs in stages. Call them ABC or the Seven Ages of Man, whatever. To me, there is first death, which comes at the close of your own childhood, and there is second death, which comes at the close of your children's childhood. And *that* death is a large part of the sadness I get now around Will and Sadie, both of whom I have loved so truly.

There is third death too, before you depart this vale of beers, but third death is hard work, it wears you drop by drop. You may have *time* before your actual physical death, or "no-moreness" as the Ojibway Indians say, but you are looking down the barrel all that time; the awful knowledge has crept on you and all the shadows are quietly haunted. So you can easily see that minus Ben Orenburg Locksley I would be well on my way tonight. Is it any wonder I have this urge to play, to romp and roll in the snow, or to contemplate in quieter moments the Rooney Plan? Locksley unlocked!

Meantime I pull the quilt right up to Benny's innocent little chin and press a kiss to his puffy cheek. He stirs a bit but I know there is nothing can wake him. Between now and dawn, Ben Franklin is about as apt to wake up as Ben O. Locksley. His mother is several fathoms down herself, though I know she will open one eye halfway if I fiddle the covers. She is having a nice sleep, her face is almost beatific, possibly she is dreaming of hazy Pennsylvania summers. Her top leg is still drawn up, hip still glazed by the muted moon-light, thigh cross-hatched by the muntin strips in the sash. I begin to untangle the sheets from between her legs and she rolls over, unconsciously aware she must soon surrender half the bed, yield up her luxurious sprawl and start to cope with the ruthless imperialism of my knees.

I smooth her lower back and rest a palm there, waiting for a sign, but Kim is still. I could probably get away without rousing her at all if I wished for that, except I am not afraid. She has had a good evening, many clues have already come to light, and when she has had one of those Kim won't care what I've done, she won't even ask. Her perfect comfort may well mean she has done some writing tonight, so I slip off the bed and tiptoe to her desk to have a gander.

A new poem! Six different drafts of it in fact, four working titles, the top copy clean and clearly finished. I am too weary to read the poem, though I can't help noting the title: The Walrus Papers. It makes me want to read the poem, but I really can't, my eyes especially are much too tired. I am content just to see the poem, happy that the poem has occurred, because for one thing it would likely not have occurred had I stayed at home. Kim has lived her life and I mine, a chapter each, and if anything she has used her time to better advantage.

"M?"

Not surprised she has stirred and called to me. I might have rummaged boisterously in the kitchen all night, or ripped apart the bedding and thrashed the quilt about her head without much disturbing her. Ten seconds I hover by her desk, however, and she is alert; and like the mother lion out scavenging near the den where her cubs are snoozing, she doubles back.

"New poem," I say.

"Hug," she says. Her arms lift, weak with sleep.

"Good one?"

AT THE HALL: KIM

"Great one," she slurs. "I feel great."

I reach beneath the blankets to play on this and report accordingly, "You *do* feel great!"

"Don't. Don't tickle, I'm sleep."

"You could wake up."

"Don't wantto wakeup."

Kim is savoring a double luxury right now, invested in the sweet heavy sleep and yet enough astir to appreciate many things at once: her work, my nearness, the physical knowledge of peace. I am slightly envious.

"The Walrus Papers?"

"Don't look yet, don't."

"Stop me."

"Don't, M."

"You stopped me."

She is satisfied by this much. She has enjoyed just the right amount of consciousness, and rolls back over into her favorite posture, halfway between her stomach and her side, one leg drawn up to form a triangle off the other, the hypotenuse. "Night," she says.

She is dreaming again by now, but I have caught the germ of her pleasure, her happiness, and I lie there alongside her nursing the glow. For the moment I have completely lost track of any confusion or discontent in my life. I am not even what I often am, a happy fella who *thinks* he's not. No, I am just plain fine. And why? Is it because I am too tired to try or to care, and happiness is like anything else, like sex or tennis or tightrope-walking, the harder you try the worse it gets? Or is it because I am not counting, as in the weary query Does Happiness Count in the face of world-wide hunger and deprivation, and isn't happiness just a petty bourgeois notion in the first place? Petty bourgeois notion in a petit bourgeois nation? Or is it because for all I know death may yet be far away?

No. Since I know the answer, I may as well be forthcoming with it. It's because Kim is happy. I have caught the germ of it as I might catch an influenza, the room is simply lousy with it. This conjugal process, these odd pairings which persist in occurring, will carry us to the grave, reader, but we are going to get there one way or another, my friends assure me. Would I seriously consider changing hearses in midstream, or was that just the momentum of the moment, back there on the floor in Somerville? Was it possibly even a form of suicide, falling on my sword in high Elizabethan style, can't eliminate Maggie then make Maggie eliminate *me* sort of elimination?

I suppose it's even possible that I am simply sloppy with drink, maudlin at Maggie's, half-seas at the Hall. It happens so rarely I tend to discount it and yet it's true I've been taking in ethyl each stop along the way. True too I find myself in a bodily state that's hard to explain, complete fatigue offset by limitless energy. I could at any millisecond fall off in mid-phrase, with my coat up under chin, and not even twitch again for twelve solid hours. Yet my mind is still whirling with memories and stories, and I could also keep after them, in the full excitement of being alive, for that same twelve hours.

To me it seems I am in the same state mentally right now as I was sexually on the stair-landing with Maggie, before I opened my big mouth and talked us out of it. Then I had the illusion we could move endlessly and smoothly, with a keen sensation that never waned or peaked, that could neither be yielded up voluntarily nor fulfill itself fully either. The very relationship I am enjoying at present with my own mind, tipsified or no!

Would it be too crazy to fetch down my overcoat and take another turn, this time solitary, on the still untrammeled snow? Do I need to "walk it off"? Maybe, but the mere thought of it gives me a shiver, taps back into my real exhaustion. My mind may be racing but my heart-beat has slowed surreally. I elect instead to take the standardized cure for restlessness within the home, the cure endorsed by every age and gender, namely opening the door to the refrigerator. Not looking for anything, you know, just seeing what is there, as on those long boring drizzly Sundays when up and down the coast every member of every family will wander to the fridge a few times, peer in, scout around, and wander away again.

In there, in the fridge, it is tap city, a mighty depressing landscape. One Kim Orenburg egg-carton (that's the kind with no eggs but with cracked shell in each of the twelve pockets), half a quart of flat beer in back, wilted lettuce in the "crisper", crumbled stinky blue-cheese in the door... She must have made the brownies with incantations in lieu of ingredients! But wait, the brownies, the balance of the brownies—Kim cannot have eaten them all, Ben was already in bed when I left. Somewhere in this house there is at least half a batch of brownies and Kim has hidden them from me because she mistrusts me, or rather because she knows me and appreciates that I could polish off the lot without blinking.

I want only one more brownie, but I want it very much. And as I forage fruitlessly in all the usual places and others less usual (on the porch, in the airshaft, in that corner of the sink cabinet we had long since abandoned to the mice), I have begun to want it absolutely, as can happen late at night with food, when there isn't any. It comes to me as it might come to Dupin or to Holmes himself, in a shock of far-fetched certainty; that vast jumble of papers on Kim's desk was too vast, too jumbled. She always creates a chaos of paper while she is working, and just as surely always puts it back in order once a poem is done. So, too clever by half, the clear copy on top is the dead giveaway.

Yes! I slide the wrapped tray of brownies out from under the cunningly arrayed layers of canary railroad manila and dart back to the safety of the kitchen just as Kim drowsily reacts to these new sounds at her desk. Neatly I cut away a single largish square and eat it. The remainder I take from the tray, re-wrap in foil, and stuff down into the laundry hamper between two shirts and a sheet. I pitch my trousers on top just to add the informal touch and then with swift sure movements replace the empty tray below Kim's crafty thatch of paper. At the most, reader, at the *most* I will extract that packet from the hamper once and I will partake of one more brownie. I may very well eat no more, not even the one, though this I could hardly be expected to guarantee, you understand.

Benny's doorway, like ours, opens off the kitchen. I say opens though it doesn't even have a door, just a curtain Kim slung up across the portal to cut off a particular slant of sunshine that wakes him with the birds in early summer. It is 3:20 now but something, perhaps just my restlessness, draws me back to his bedside for a final peek. Benny has not moved. He is still sprawled against the safe embankment of the far wall, his little arms still flung up over his little head. Again I lean down to kiss his pretty face (sweet dreams, white) and abruptly, in yet another split-second invasion of the senses, I recall an episode that took place thirty years ago in my home town. Not merely recall it, either—I reclaim it whole, I *relive* it in total heartfreezing detail. And so must you then; it's another bit of my boyhood, first life before the first death, another blast from the past for you.

It may well have been precisely thirty years ago tonight, because it did occur in the week before Christmas, certainly within a day or two of this date. And the world was well under snow that night too, though it made a different picture, for the town was not large, there were not so many cars, and even on the main street there were large sweeping elm trees and maples. But that night while my pals and I carelessly slept, a girl from our classroom lay seriously ill at her home near the center of the village. I don't know what her disease was perceived to be, I never heard, and I don't know why she wasn't in a hospital bed either, although at that time much more illness was conducted in the home and much more dying as well. And this girl Phoebe, whom I knew quite well, having shared a desk with her one year and a classroom three years running, was indeed in danger of dying, though she was barely ten years old and though none of us who knew her at school had the slightest inkling it could happen.

Phoebe's father stayed in the room with her that whole night, apparently, in a state of nervous exhaustion and incipient madness no doubt. Who after all can say why it is, or how, we humans agree to control ourselves at moments when our loss and grief are deepest; how we keep from lashing out in fury or wailing in endless lament when death so facelessly extinguishes a life that has been part of our own. In the case of Phoebe's father, that mechanism of control was not there, or it was not working.

Doctor Brooks, whom I recall as a large and friendly man, had been at Phoebe's side for seven hours himself, outlasting two nurses, calling for ice to stop the fever, and penicillin, but reality proved too cruel and she failed steadily. Sometime past midnight, the doctor was forced to announce, in a bereavement of his own, that she was in fact dead. At once Phoebe's father shoved him back from her bedside and screamed in the man's face he was a liar. He shunted aside his wife, who sought to hold him, and when she persisted nearly threw her to the floor. "She isn't dead!" he cried. "Phoebe isn't dead!"

No doubt the child looked little different that moment from the moment previous, no doubt that for now only an expert could know for sure that uncommon coldness which so quickly replaces the fever. The distance between life and death is a millionth of a second in time: the heart beats, the heart has stopped beating. It is a finer and finer line as it approaches and yet no philosopher could ever take in the vast irreversible distance in *kind* it signals. The finality, the absolute and eternal void that looms, makes too great a shock. Even in the electric death-house, when some sub-human fiend who has carved a dozen women into small pieces is at last put to death himself, when death might be seen by some as "good", the most hardened souls, the most ardent executionists feel this shock — not the literal one but the shock of space between the instant when the criminal watches and waits and the next instant, when he no longer exists at all.

"Phoebe isn't dead!" her father shouted, lifting her body from the bed and stumbling out into the streets of the village. Up the main street he ran, cradling his daughter in his arms and crying, over and over again, "Phoebe isn't dead, she isn't dead!" The police arrived, the fire engine and the ambulance, and clusters of people soon gathered in spite of the hour. They all stood dumbfounded and watched him, coatless in the December cold, his frail tragic child so lovingly enfolded, until finally he collapsed in the shallow snow, weeping, and was led away. The Chief of Police carried Phoebe back home to her mother, separate but equal victim of the same precise shock, waiting in numbed silence.

And I recall the talk that went around at school the next day among the ten-year-old children who had been Phoebe's peers. She had suddenly become a nervous joke. It was somehow *funny* the way her dad had carried on, funny even that she was dead. I was greeted that morning by crooked smiles and odd conspiratorial laughter; had I "heard the news", Phoebe was dead. To me, and to the others as well, it was absolutely stunning and unanswerable, grief too naked and sorrow too helpless to face. It was too much to take in and though we couldn't help hearing the details as they emerged, we all put it quickly behind us, as though Phoebe had never existed. What became of the father I never learned, nor the mother. Until this night, thirty years later, I had not thought once of that night, and yet I have it as clear as if it were transpiring right now, in this room.

A sentimental tale? You bet. Dickens told many such a sentimental story, and drew forth many an honest tear. And what of little Ilusha in Dostoevsky's saga of the Karamozovs? You object to the heart-tugging use of the adjective "little"? Well the boy weighed sixty pounds or so, shall we term him otherwise? I bend yet again and place another sentimental kiss on Benny's soft cheek, a sentimental gesture from a sentimental man (Hello, Locksley here!), and I cover again, for the second time in twenty minutes, the third time tonight, his strong round shoulders, and I have found another reason to be happy: Benny isn't dead.

# THE APATHY OF THE STARS

I can appreciate that by now you have tired of watching me wander around the house at this ungodly hour, and if you'll only kiss me goodnight, reader, I am ready to close out my account of the evening. It is done anyway and though it has been at times elliptical, I think the essentials have settled between the ellipses and that you know me now, well enough. What follows, pour l'envoi, is a last fragment from my youth that is this time a fragment from every man's youth, and that may show you how I am feeling at the end of this night, how I feel at the end of most nights, and maybe how you feel too.

Possibly the phenomenon has ceased to exist, or exists only in the tank-towns of the south and mid-west now, but not too long ago, back before pornography supplanted bread and milk as the staples at Paul's Variety, a young man often encountered his first naked woman (other than kin) or hoped to encounter her, at the carnival on the edge of town. There was always the stripper, advertised chiefly by word of mouth (for she was surely in violation of some local ordinance) always the late groundswell to mosey on out and see her act, what the hell, and the scene would have an almost lyrical dreariness about it.

The small bulbs strung together in the autumn wind, the tired calliope's gallop, the pockmarked barker at the front fold of the waterstained tent... And the stories! She would take a lit cigarette and puff on it with the lips of her vagina; she would solicit a pair of eye-glasses from someone in the front row and cause them to disappear, only to squeeze them back out and offer snifters. To a tribe of wide-eyed teenage boys, and yes Virginia they were still pretty wide-eyed back then, this prospect was in equal measure gross, mysterious, and alluring. They had to want to see it and so there they stood, inside the grubby tent on a grassy floor, the rye field mowed or merely trampled down, and they weren't seeing the grubby tent or the rye field where just last week they may have tossed a football. They saw only the promise of revelation, mystery demystified.

The cigarette, the eye-glasses—it wasn't that these things couldn't happen, but they didn't, praise God, and by the time every myth was demythified no one cared anymore, for the deflationary process had been slow and thorough. At first there was nothing, just the eagerness, and the joking, and the long wait. Then out came the musician, a singer accompanying himself on ukelele or mandolin, performing showboat tunes or perhaps a leering bawdy sea-shanty. He sang and he danced a bit until at last the "receptive audience" became what they had really been all along, a gang of overgrown sarcastic children, and they started in riding him with mounting animal impatience.

Finally the hook would take him off, and then there would be more waiting, quite a bit more, until at last, with a subtle shading of the single forty-watt bulb and a pathetic fanfare from the scratchy little phonograph in plain view on the platform stage, out she came, paunch and all. Fifty years old, maybe fifty-five, heavily rouged from head to toe and, beneath her layers of fringed and tattered silk, with pasties as big as beer-coasters and a ratty G-string that one might later become nostalgically grateful for, when in much stealth and darkness it did actually come away...

Life, to pontificate a bit, is a lot like that show to me and as I muse back over the evening we have just shared, I can attest that I felt this most keenly as I drove away from Rockland Terrace, and watched Maggie Cornelius loping over the snow, and stopped at the foot of her hill to gather my emotions. Life does tease us, it throws its grubby tents up around us, and for the short time we're inside we don't see the grubbiness and drear, we see only the promise of the show we've come to enjoy. When the show is over we are disappointed, because it wasn't good, and yet at the same time there is a feeling of relief, that it wasn't *worse*. That it's over and you're *still there*. You step outside onto the midway again and the air is still shining, the moon sails west.